Dorian

JEREMY REED

Dorian

PETER OWEN
London & Chester Springs PA

PETER OWEN PUBLISHERS
73 Kenway Road London SW5 0RE
Peter Owen books are distributed in the USA by
Dufour Editions Inc. Chester Springs PA 19425–0007

First published in Great Britain 1997
© Jeremy Reed 1997

ISBN 0 7206 1012 5

A catalogue record for this book is available from
the British Library

Printed and bound in Great Britain by
Biddles Ltd, Guildford and King's Lynn

For Annie MacLean

Preface

THIS novel begins where Wilde's ends. *Dorian* creates a fictional continuity for the figure of Dorian Gray, the renowned protagonist of Oscar Wilde's *The Picture of Dorian Gray*.

My Dorian has survived the laceration of his portrait and escaped to Paris, where we find him living with Lord Henry Wotton. The book is not intended as a literal sequel to Wilde's novel, but more as the expansion of a theme into its modern equivalents. I have taken liberties with the time-frame, and juxtaposed historic with contemporary associations. I have tried to maintain the spirit of Wilde's authoritatively decadent novel, and to transpose his *fin de siècle* aesthetics to a corresponding set of values existing at the end of the twentieth century. The figure of Dorian Gray will always remain as the archetype for a sort of youth which, while it outwardly appears to resist the process of age, is inwardly corrupt and irredeemable.

Youth and age, innocence and experience, these are the perennial themes of art. In giving Dorian Gray another face-lift, I have not altered the predominant characteristics with which Wilde invested his creation. It is quite simply another time, another place, and so the story continues.

J.R.

Chapter 1

FROM where he sat, head tilted back in a blue velvet chair, left arm thrown out perpendicular to his body, while the right supported a book in his lap, Dorian could make out the couple in the window opposite his apartment in the Rue de Rivoli. Their ritual was inveterately sustained, and it had become a distraction too for Harry to engage in the voyeuristic stimulus of watching an act of exhibitionistic transvestism. They were a couple. And at first Dorian had mistaken the blond one for a woman, the face articulated by light, with pronounced make-up, the line of the skirt reproachfully tight, all the feminine over-compensations crowding for attention. This person's part-ner was waspishly tall, with a defined waist and shoulders, his dark hair gelled off the forehead, his various pick-me-out-in-the-crowd black suits exact in their symmetrically aligned creases. As a couple, they kept apart in the street, and Dorian had ob-served their instinctual caution in screening each other from any random contact with a stranger's body.

What he had seen by chance one night, through the uncurtained window of a brightly lit apartment, was very similar to what he found himself watching now. He called Harry over to his view-ing-point, and the latter, who had been fluffing out a display of pink and red carnations, took up a position next to Dorian which afforded direct visual access to the opposite window. The ritual of the one undressing the other was rehearsed with such

9

practised, slow-motion technique that Dorian assumed the participants got their stimulus from their provocatively public display.

The one who cross-dressed was standing facing Dorian, and was partly bending over the chair on which he would later stand naked. The other's preoccupying fascination with unlacing the tie-ribbons of a black waspie was so intense that Dorian could almost feel the concentrated energy beam directed by the man's sensory instruction. His method was teasingly slow, and it seemed a rule of the game that neither broke a preconceived discipline. If the unlacing occupied a period of twenty minutes, the divestiture of boots and silk stockings was a similarly protracted affair, the culmination of the strip being the removal of two red frou-frou garters.

Dorian and Harry had watched the precision performance thirty times over during the past three months, and neither had tired of this act of studiously perfected eroticism. It served as an aphrodisiac, and as a stimulating subtext to their own perverse erotic imagery. Dorian knew that at a precise point in the proceedings Harry would come over and surprise him with the roughness or softness of his touch. His fingertips, inserted in the interstice between his shirt buttons, would describe circles round his nipples, before dropping to his waist.

Sometimes when Dorian looked up and saw Lord Henry Wotton, or Harry, so centrally a part of his life, his heart dropped a beat in the apprehension of love and fear. Dorian had often reflected on the ambivalent twist in their relationship, and how their love was fed by the inverse proportion of hatred that bound them together. Each knew too much about the other, and on Harry's first coming to join Dorian in Paris, an act in defiance of his marriage and social status, Dorian had rewarded his temerity by telling Harry the full story of the murders he had committed before disappearing into exile. His confessions shocked his listener, especially because of the air of detachment with which he narrated his preconceived crimes. And at no point, either in the perpetration of the crimes, or in his retrospective evaluation of them as cold narrative, had Dorian appeared connected to his actions. His radical dissociation from reality was a continuous source of disquiet to Lord Henry. And what Dorian realised in his private hours, crossing the city at random in the late afternoon, was his isolation in time. He had eluded pursuit by the authorities, but he lived with the apprehension that an undercover agent trailed him through the foggy boulevards. At other times he imagined that his crimes were known to an underground coterie, and that on his entry to a bar in the early hours of the morning, the entire clientele would rise holding candles, and without saying a word judge him by their collective stare. Blue eyes, brown eyes, green eyes, grey eyes, their magnitude would freeze him, and if he ran back to the street they would pursue like a speeded-up cortège, each of them dressed in black and carrying a gun in the right hand.

Sometimes Dorian would enter a maze of alleys in Montmartre or Pigalle convinced that somewhere in the anonymous streets was a house in which his victims sat waiting to forgive him. They had never really died, only sleepwalked a little into a parallel dimension, and then returned to invisible living. Basil Hallward would be sitting in a pool of sunlight on the studio floor, and his age would be thirty-five and there would be no sign of injuries to his body. His white shirt would be open at the collar, a red necktie escaping down the front, and when he looked up he would see through pain and see nothing. In his state of bilocated consciousness he would be somewhere else other than in Dorian's reality. And Dorian's illegitimate half-brother, Jim, would be sitting in another corner of the room, turning over the stones on his fingers, and looking blankly at Basil's back, as though he were locating him in a dream that would abruptly shift its visual field. On seeing Dorian he would with gestural articulacy take off the rings that Dorian had placed on his fingers after killing him, and component by component dematerialise. It was Dorian's obsession that, once he had discovered this house, he would return in search of it every day. Blood would sweat from its walls, and in time a family would come back from a long vacation abroad to reclaim their property. There would be house lights on at night, and two white coffins with black crosses assembled on the front steps.

This was the sort of recurrent hallucination that Dorian

experienced, even in the snatches of voyeuristic intensity, when excited by his blond neighbour's male genitalia emerging from black silk panties, he lost bits of his tormented fixations, and entered into the immediacy of the sexual exhibitionism on display. Usually the couple drew the curtains after their delayed prelude to sex, and left it to their spectators to imagine the positioning of their bodies on the bed, but this time they went at it in full light. Renouncing all pretence at disinterested observation, Dorian went over to the window and pressed his face up against the glass in his eagerness to capture moments of their love-making. Encouraged by his example, Harry also came to the window and angled his head impossibly in an attempt to make out the entangled geometry of two bodies lost to the eye by reason of the positioning of their mattress on the floor. Dorian could make out the struggle of silhouettes on the far wall, and then, agonised by the frustration of being unable to see, he withdrew back to his chair, leaving Harry to quiz the window agitatedly.

The air between the two of them simmered with undercurrents. It could snap as easily into a violent altercation as it could into sexual energy. There was a zingy disharmony in the air, like a summer storm kicking up on the skyline for hours before it broke into brilliant torrential rain. Harry had been showing all the signs of being stretched taut. A year of smouldering understated recriminations had left its mark. Clandestine letters to his wife, and, as Dorian suspected, casual sexual liaisons with boys introduced to him by the ruined poet, Paul Verlaine, had instated in him a nervy, mistrustful sensibility. Harry's cool, the diplomatic suavity of his disposition, had been distributed into a jumpy, fragmented expression under strain of a double life. Dorian knew that Harry had never quite let go of his wife, and that a side of him resented his fall into a privileged but *déclassé* exile under an assumed name. Dorian had grown able to pick out the breakage-points in Harry, the areas of strain as they were recorded in his body. They were like the fingerstops on a damaged organism.

Harry came back from the window and folded himself elegantly in a chair. Dorian sensed that Harry wanted to go on one of his nocturnal forays into the city's bad areas, clandestine social dates, the dinners at Le Roux, from which he, Dorian, was always excluded. It was either that or the risk of explosion. The excitement opposite was over, and Harry needed renewed excitement.

'Shall I come with you, Harry?' Dorian anticipated, forcing the tension.

'What do you mean by that?' Harry questioned, his voice immediately defensive.

'Wasn't it you who told me on your own admission that you colour sin only with danger. Or engage in what Oscar called "feasting with panthers" as the only real colour element left in life?'

'You take me too seriously,' Harry replied, detaching himself from the conversation, and staring abstractedly into space. He was anxious to get out into the city and to be alone. The rhythm of walking, and just letting accidental encounters happen, was for him relief from the volume of tension that existed at home. Harry wished he knew less about Dorian's shadow. In the initial intensity of their relationship, each had been recklessly indiscriminate about what to make a shared knowledge. Now it seemed to Harry that Dorian's two murders floated in his eyeballs. Sometimes he could see his old friend Basil Hallward staring out of Dorian's left eye, while the right reddened with the exhibit of the crime which had taken them first to Europe and finally to Paris.

Harry left the apartment, knowing that he would return to find Dorian either drugged or drunk. Dorian made no secret of the opium habit he had developed over the last four years in London, and in Paris he had found dens the equivalent of the Limehouse ones in London. Dorian smoked at home, and Harry would often return late at night to find Dorian sitting up, almost cataleptic in his distraction. The paralysing visuals of his autonomous stream of consciousness left Dorian exhausted, nervous, and at times emaciated. And then he would undergo a brief detoxification in a private clinic, kick the habit for a number of months, only to be inexorably hooked again. It was tiring for both of them. Dorian couldn't help himself, and Harry was too preoccupied with his own problems to be of assistance. He knew that Dorian was buying the drug from somewhere else other than pharmacies, and was most likely getting it on the street, or making in-house purchases from the Chinese dens.

Outside, there was a mist blowing in from the river, and the autumnal air was chilled like a wine brought to just the right temperature. Harry liked the contained bite in the air. The lights were on all over town, and the pit of his stomach tightened. It was Dorian's hour of the wolf, the time when the underworld surfaced, and a night vocabulary became written into the nerves. Harry was compelled to keep up vestiges of social pretensions. Dorian would compare the sexual outlaw's journey to heroic descent into the underworld. The day-world ritualistically reversed itself into a network of sexual contacts. It was a left-handed, left-sided microcosm in which Dorian walked in reflection on his wound. Harry had, by natural instinct, refrained from entering into that viciously contaminated ethos. There was a room beneath the city supported by jet columns, all the furniture was black, and there was a huge wooden cross in it, from which the willing S & M victim would hang. Harry had heard of this place from Dorian, and tonight he resolved to check out the club's notorious fetishistic practices. Near him was the night river, smelling of rainstorms, effluvia, oil and solitude. Harry had come to think of that stretch of water as the passage between life and death, in the way the separation between the living and the dead appeared to be one of speech. He knew Dorian visited that underground room in order to realise his shadow. Dorian had opened up the way for him, and he had been shocked on listening at first to discover the pathologised aspect of his psyche, and then, hungry to pursue its need, he had grown fascinated by stories about the place. At times he feared he was becoming too much like Dorian, and when the mood was on him he resented the latter's insidious means of infiltrating his psyche. He cursed him in other company, and then guilty of his actions he returned to him for security and consolation. His destroyer was also his healer.

It was in his night visits to cafés and restaurants that Harry had come across the drunken, dissolute figure of Paul Verlaine, only to find of course that Dorian had already made the poet's acquaintance. And from Verlaine, with his propensity for low life, Harry had first heard of the visionary pyrotechnics of Arthur Rimbaud, and of the brief years of their hysterical liaison, spent on the road, or in desperate poverty in cities. Harry had heard of Rimbaud's fantastically innovative poetry, of his extreme idealism, and of the imaginative principles on which he had hoped to found a new reality. Verlaine had spoken with alternate love and contempt for his dead friend, who had died in Marseille in 1891 when he was about to set off for Abyssinia. He hadn't seen Rimbaud in twenty years, but he was proud of the consecrated scar on his right palm, where Rimbaud had driven a knife in one of their violent altercations. He presented his wound as palpable evidence of their once turbulent friendship. Verlaine drank glass after glass of absinthe, and with a self-annihilative rapacity which had fetched him up on the streets, or driven him for periods in winter into hospitals. His undignified dipsomania had rendered him squat, lame and decrepit, but he had never quite relinquished his memories of having been a poet, and of having engaged in a tempestuous relationship with a provincial schoolboy invested with poetic genius.

Verlaine inhabited workers' cafés. His eyes shifted dimension as the water was poured over the sugar cubes in the sieve, and the absinthe clouded green. His hand moved independent of his thoughts, and as Harry threaded a series of nocturnal alleys towards a bar where he knew the poet would be drinking, so he remembered that hand's jerky, nervous mechanism. Verlaine needed to feed his nerves with the fairy with green eyes. It was as if he drank always to outstrip the past, and, never sure if the road was catching up on him, he tried by drinking more to obliterate its existence. Perhaps it was Rimbaud's footsteps he heard. Rimbaud had run across the face of the earth in his old leather boots, bashed in at the toes, and would never let up in his pursuit.

Harry found Verlaine slumped at a table in Le Procope. The poet's natural demeanour was one of glowering truculence, a mood that side-shifted to a tear-splashed moroseness, or a jocular obscenity. He was sitting next to a blue-denimed worker, whose

femininity showed in his long eyelashes, and in the self-conscious
manner in which he dipped his eyes when speaking. The boy
couldn't have been more than twenty, and there was confusion
in the way his developed musculature and crude manners contrasted with feminine eyes. He was called Lucien. Lucien Letinois.
Verlaine was quick to make it known to Harry, under his breath,
that Lucien would be right for Dorian.

Verlaine sometimes played the role of pimp, and purveyed
street-boys in return for money to buy absinthe. And Harry,
who was in part repulsed by his similar descent into a world of
incompatible pick-ups, involuntarily tensed with tormenting jealousy to think that this boy had been procured to please his
lover. The café was a blue fuzz of smoke, and Verlaine with his
broad, truncated nose, his ferrety eyes hidden by caterpillar
eyebrows, and his sensual mouth, was already half blasted by
alcohol. His head rocked on its axis. He looked like someone
whose mind was filling up with blue ice-floes. He came at the
immediate from a long way back, and his speech was furred.
He had probably been cooking his brain all day to a series of
fried craters.

Lucien was initially shy of Harry, whose naturally fastidious
reserve shone through his attempts to read the atmosphere and
be absorbed by his surroundings. Lucien worked in one of the
riverside warehouses. He smelt of the sacks of coffee-beans he
lifted all day, and the evidence of his work was in the beam of
his shoulders. He was largely inarticulate, his gestures rather
than his words pointing up the ideas he intended to express.
Lucien's energies were emphatically physical, but it was the feminine side of him, unchoreographed by nuances of language,
that captivated Harry. The boy would probably never achieve
unity of gender, and so he was angular, potentially violent and
fiercely defensive of his masculinity. He drank with commitment, but unlike Verlaine his preference was for red wine rather
than absinthe. He was less done-in than the older man, but
showed alarming lateral shifts towards chaos. They were both
skirting black interior holes.

Verlaine was in a mood to reminisce, no matter how
disconnectedly. He sensed in Harry someone sympathetic to

the buried vestiges of the poet in him. His fineness seemed to have been extracted from him like the spinal bone of a fish. The rest of the man had grown insensitively crusty, and his holed greatcoat was the colour of an alley. He talked of Mathilde, the girl he had married when she was eighteen and pregnant. 'I dragged her upstairs by her hair and laid her out on the bed,' he said to Lucien for the other's approval. 'I enjoyed a change of sex' when Rimbaud arrived, he confided, and narrated the story of Rimbaud's first letters and poems sent by him from Charleville, and of his arrival in Paris. He spoke of Rimbaud's peasant body, his big bony hands, his defiant idealism, and of his blue eyes, the sort of blue, Verlaine said, that is to be found in southern skies. Harry still hadn't read Rimbaud's poems, but Verlaine could quote whole passages from *Les Illuminations* and *Une Saison en Enfer*, and surprised Harry by Rimbaud's adjectival use of primary colours, and of the volatile implosiveness of his imagery. Verlaine was insistent that Rimbaud had altered the way we see the universe, but that it would take a long time for people to figure that out. In his mind, and in jumpy, incohesive flashes Verlaine was out on the country roads again, tramping the yellow woods with Rimbaud, sleeping in a farm outhouse, or walking at a fast lick on the high road to somewhere, anywhere, nowhere.

Warming to Harry's evident homoeroticism, Lucien approved of Rimbaud's having taken Verlaine from his wife. 'The arsehole's only a cunt turned back to front,' he volunteered, the wine running out of his loaded cheeks as if from a split ruby.

Harry thought of his own wife and was not amused. He swallowed hard on the memory of once having played the part of misogynist to Dorian. Now he doubted his earlier resolve and fitted his teeth into his nether lip. Sometimes he would do that until he tasted blood. Life with Dorian had taught him that a man could not double for a woman, and if he had been hoping to find a surrogate wife in his male lover, then he would go disappointed. Dorian had proved inflexibly and indomitably cold, and unable to love women; he had looked to revenge himself in his sexual relations with men. His cruelty had come close to breaking Harry, but love, which also asserted the fascination to be ruined by the other, still drove him back to Dorian's company, no matter he cursed the man blue in private rages.

Verlaine was lit by an irrational flush. His feet were swollen and he looked terminally cirrhotic. Harry perceived that the man would die in the near future. Marks of his discreditable homicidal rages were redly tracked in his eyes. Harry could not imagine how a man so damaged by alcohol could perform sexually. Yet it was clear that the bond between Verlaine and Lucien was sexual. Each would place a hand on the other's knee when animated by a shared, brutal obscenity. Harry came to this café on his way to the underground club. In the latter he expected to find some young man up on the cross, his body responsive to every hit. S & M *aficionados* would come and go throughout the night, masonic initiates to the whip and the rack. Men from all walks of life in Paris would arrive secretly, some of them choosing to conceal their identity by the adoption of leather masks, while others he knew would be open about the need that drove them to the underworld. Harry was aware of the risk of a raid on the premises but was compelled out of a perverse agency to keep on visiting the club.

And all over the town that day, on the billboards, was the news of Oscar Wilde's conviction, subsequent to his having instigated proceedings against the Marquess of Queensberry. Wilde's sexual practices were common knowledge, but the interference of the law brought a collective chill to Dorian's world, as though a hidden nerve-point had been alerted to pain. All day Harry had seen his shadow, he had been jerked into a cold sweat by sensing the tangible presence of a double. And what if others could see it too? Dorian would not care about such things. He was sold to a degree of self-destruction by which he delighted in the acceleration of the process. Dorian's shadow was black on black. It was invisible.

Harry left Verlaine, with Lucien's address copied out by the poet on a square of paper for Dorian. Harry felt his own duplicitous sense of corruption in indirectly purveying for Dorian, and there was the beginning of a resolve in him to rid himself of the whole matter. It was as though he had tasted dark and swallowed it as pungent grit. And now the night air had a different tang, not the singed crispness of a particular seasonal clarity, but more what he was anticipating – the reek of leather bitten by whips, and the scent of ritualised punishment as it was voiced through perversely incantational octaves.

Harry heard a barge go down the night river. There were bouncers at the entrance to the underground steps. They were dressed all in leather, with made-up eyes and shaved heads. Harry pulled back from immediate entrance to the club and inhaled the river air. He wanted to delay his moment of transitional identity and evaluate the schizoid within himself. Each time he mixed with low company he assured himself it would be the last. There was still latitude for a reconciliation with his wife, and a chance to reintegrate with normal society. The compulsion to be with Dorian, and to risk possible arrest as an habitué of the nocturnal underworld, was an attraction he knew would end in degradation and ruin. Suddenly he caught a whiff of vetiver, and it was a clean, instructive association, an imaginary link between himself and a moment in his youth. He realised the scent was imaginary, but it was a psychological prompting to reconsider.

The river was just below the parapet on which he stood. It was a black snake with jumpy neons lozenging its back. Water smelt of memory. Something you could never grasp but which was always immediate. He could hear conspiratorial voices coming up from a landing-bay on a jetty. There were always night people, those whose metabolism lived in reverse, and who discoursed in the big black silence the night afforded. The left-sided, deformative ones who sat in cafés or bars until dawn, and the visionaries who sensed change in the night, and the coming closer of a new ethos. Harry had walked the night to hide the unease in himself which would have been evident by day. He knew he could not return direct to his wife. He had become someone else in his time away, and the shadow side of that character had to be integrated before he could resume a married relationship. He had grown to be jerky, and terrified of what he encountered on the inside. Had he not once said to Dorian, 'I am so steeped in evil that there is no action of yours which will ever prove comfortable. I represent all the sins you have never had the courage to commit'? At the time he had projected the image of someone who lived dangerously, and now, standing above the night river, his skin tingling with the impact of slow, flashy raindrops, he had reason to reflect on how he was growing to be the embodiment of his fantasy. And if Dorian's life-style had outstripped his own fascination with evil, it had none the less accelerated his own dealings with the underworld. He had at first felt compelled to compete with and challenge his prodigy, and had taken on the role of psychological accomplice to actions that repulsed him. Dorian had not only liquidated his oldest friend, Basil Hallward, but in a crazy scheme to cover his tracks, he had murdered his own illegitimate half-brother, placed his own rings on the dead man's defaced body, and so effectively given rise to the belief that Dorian Gray was dead. The latter was statistically supposed to have been cremated, and the scandal surrounding his freakish extension of youth, silenced. Dorian had never been properly accepted as a reality; rather, people preferred to think of him as an absent dimension, a void, or someone who never happened. With his death he had been demythicised, as though everything about him had belonged to missing time. There was the suspicion perhaps that even if Dorian had shifted from three-dimensional physical perception to two-dimensional psychic reflection, he might perhaps continue to infiltrate as a post-biological presence. People wanted to pretend that he had neither lived nor died, but Harry was actually sharing an apartment with a man who still showed little sign of physically ageing, and who appeared cut off from most human emotions.

The rain was coming on. He could hear it tripping on the river's back with waspish persistence. He did not care, but stood there a long time looking out at its moving columns. He was waiting for the bright dot in his brain cells, a sign that would show him the way. He thought of it sometimes as a door opening in the sky, a white rectangle set into the black curve of space. Time would not exist in that zone, just the clarity of a resolved dilemma shining through in its right context.

The rain quickened to a uniform smudge, cancelling out the opposite bank. Harry walked back towards the club entrance, disappointed yet again that he had failed to pinpoint an option in his conflicting programme of choices. If only the light in his head would come clear, he would know what to do and how to do it. And it was becoming an obsessive nightly ritual, this waiting for the inner flash to occur. He took himself in the direction of the club, for there he was determined to lose himself. Illumination could come anywhere and burn holes in the moment.

The place was beginning to fill up. The air was dense with woody cologne, smoke, the overload of voices scratching to be heard, and the stage was being prepared for a torch singer's entrée, a sequinned diva who would sing of tears and traumas to an audience sold on discipline and in for the kill. Harry disguised himself by adopting a leather mask on entrance. The smokescreen effects of dry ice partially obscured the S & M pack of transvestites, gays and voyeuristic spectators, police informers and serious weirdos who had collected in the big underground room, its ceiling lit by gold stars. A transvestite dressed in nothing but a red boa and leather hot pants fitted himself up against Harry before disappearing back to the fetishist crowd. Harry exchanged the aphoristic cynicism he had cultivated for dinner parties for a terse, noncommittal mode of expression better suited to his new milieu. His aim was to deflect attention from his person, and to impersonalise all exchanges with new contacts. He viewed himself with the objective eye of a spectator. His dissociation suggested he was a stand-in for a way of life he had not fully assimilated.

The torch singer had come on cradling red roses. She dripped with jewellery in a solitary spotlight, her voice colouring dramatic arias of loss, and her arms thrown up high to emphasise the tragic vulnerability of the unrequited lover. She was accompanied by a pianist on the ebony Bechstein, the whole melodramatic performance being over-stylised. She exited after three songs, and Harry found himself moving from one section of the crowd to another, not knowing what he was looking for but none the less searching. People had clearly grouped themselves according to their sexual preferences and were striking up liaisons for future contact. Harry knew from Dorian, and other acquaintances, that men risked their reputations in this night inside another night. Harry was waiting for the luminous flash that would instruct him how to proceed. There was a fast exhilarating rush in the air. People were being turned on by pain and all its sensory associations. Harry kept moving in closer on the scenes of action, his natural caution keeping a fractional check on his instincts. The place was divided into a network of connecting rooms, and different practices were being carried out according to the sectioning. The big room was reserved for the cross and the willing victim who would mount it as a climax to the building tension. Somebody would be led to it, hidden beneath a hooded red cloak, and would be assisted into position. He had listened to Dorian recounting this performance. And still people streamed in out of the rainy Paris night, the deep night now, for the hours were flying and Harry guessed it must be three or four in the morning. That dead still hour in which the world seemed to stop turning. The time of the empire of dreams setting up in the unconscious.

The place was suddenly silent. The atmospherics suggested the victim was about to be led in. The lights dropped. Harry could make out the scarlet-cloaked figure being escorted into the room by four masked assistants. The procession made its ceremonial way towards the cross, the victim carrying an air of privilege at his being the chosen one. Harry tensed at the onset of the proceedings. He worked his gloved fingers together. He was not sure what he was doing there, other than that it fulfilled an insatiable need to rival Dorian. His nerve had snapped. If the fear in coming here had generated excitement, that fear was proving corrosively counterproductive and Harry knew he risked cracking if he pushed himself beyond his own limits.

When the red cloak was removed from the victim's shoulders, he was seen to be slim, with an exceptional figure. He had his back to the spectators, but Harry was sure he knew him. Dressed in a body stocking and mask, the figure was placed in handcuffs and subjected to the whip-hand of each of four attendants. Their severity was unmodulated. Risk impacted the crowd. This was no ordinary victim on the cross, but someone trained in the disciplinary protocol. His needs were quite beyond those of his disciplinarians. There was a dignity to his masochism that made him invincible by humiliation.

Harry felt himself charged with excitement. He pushed his way towards the front of the crowd. The dense attack of spectators seemed collectively to inhale and exhale according to the action. The young man on the cross was indomitable. He was beyond pain and situated somewhere in a neutral mental space. When the four attendants had exhausted their whip-hands, they removed themselves from the crowd and disappeared into a private room, leaving the victim respite before undergoing the next phase of discipline. No one spoke, a reverential and complicitous silence pushed round the boundaries of the room. People bit on the rims of their glasses – and drained the spirit contents.

After a short interval a black man wearing a mauve feathered mask, his built-up pectorals and musculature bulking on his frame, walked through the crowd, whip in hand, and knelt before his victim. He kissed the handle of his bull-whip and lifted it like an offering. Harry guessed that this would prove the finale to the night, an unsparing sadism directed at an equally extreme masochism. Something within Harry did not want to believe the identity of the victim, and he blanked out the image that kept recurring in his mind. After this last ritualised act he would leave, walk out into the sobering dawn rain, and take a cab home.

The man got up from his genuflected posture and raised himself to full height. He looked like someone who could break a concrete pillar at one cut. The reverb from his first lash was a dull, whistling, sonic authority. A coarser skin was meeting a softer pigment, and Harry found himself involuntarily swallowing at the ferocity of the lash. To the listener it seemed impossible to withstand that brutal force. The concentrated exertion had the black man pour with sweat. A second lash resounded through the room, followed in quick succession by a third and a fourth. The volley came back at the spectators like a thunderwhack. Harry felt himself forcibly blown off his axis. The victim remained soundless, as though disengaged from physical pain and really not present. The lack of any response on his part increased the sadist's frustration, and the man tore at him with unrestrained licence. The set of his face accentuated the resolve he felt to annihilate his victim.

Then suddenly it was all over. The man threw down his whip, had a red cloak placed over his shoulders, and withdrew from the room. What appeared unaccountable to Harry was that the victim showed no signs of scarring. He had remained implacable throughout. At a note from the piano, the four original attendants came back through the crowd and made for the man on the cross. They approached him with deference, two of them releasing him from his upper shackles, and the other two supporting his lower body weight, one of them slipping a red cloak over his exhausted body. They turned him round slowly to face the crowd, and as they did so his mask slipped. In a moment of shocking revelation Harry recognised Dorian's face, his eyes closed, a rusty scratch of blood trickling from his lips. Too enervated to stand, Dorian was escorted through the stunned audience to a private room.

Harry watched the floor become the ceiling, then the ceiling the floor. He was displaced, and had to right his spin. Unable to appease the spectrum of his perversity, Dorian had become the leather-crowned king of the underworld. The red-cloaked S & M apotheosis, conjecture of whose identity would lead to the creation of a legendary figure in the pantheon of twisted gods. A man bleeding with roses as a hieroglyphic alphabet.

Harry went outside into the early morning rain, the quick hits dabbing at his skin. He felt brutally shocked, terrorised, and in need of separating from his past. He longed for solitary discourse with the river. He had seen the man for whom he had sacrificed his reputation situated in the context of a debased ritual. Harry had failed to achieve love with either sex, but the gravitation to go back to his wife was stronger than the apprehension he felt at becoming a split-off of Dorian's irreversible pull towards self-destruction. And as he walked aimlessly in no direction he remembered ideas he had expounded without ever realising their implications. It came back to him how he had repeatedly told Dorian and his circle that he considered conformism to represent a failure to cultivate self-awareness. And while he still believed in revolution on an inner plane, he questioned the relationship of ideas to actions. He was in a void, and the absence of love in his life was impressed on him by his picking a course along the river at daybreak. The river's grey eye had swallowed history. It was an indifferent loop constantly played back on itself.

Harry threaded his way through streets he had never known before, and in each one he saw Dorian's red-cloaked figure up against a wall, or tied to a lamppost, like the sacrificial and dying god. The image was an obsessive one; it kept on repeating like a single film frame. He needed help for his shredded nerves. His wife's face swam in close. He nurtured the illusory belief that she could and would take him back. When a cab appeared through the early morning rain, he flagged it down and headed for the apartment.

It was a solitary experience, coming back as always to no one. The bedroom was heady with its perfume overload. There were books everywhere, and Dorian's more secret ones were locked away in a concealed room adjoining the bedroom. Red and pink carnations watched him opaquely with mad eyes. He felt that everywhere he looked he would find evidence of Dorian's schizoid life. Or perhaps there were multiple lives. Dorian 1, 2, 3, 4, 5, 6, all the way to a thousand. Harry lay down on the bed and looked up at the stars on the ultramarine ceiling. Dorian, who lived only by night, had the bedroom resemble a galactic *annus mirabilis*. In their entire time in Paris he had hardly ever ventured out into the day. He had lost all touch with reality, and Harry too had begun to drift the same way, returning home at dawn and sleeping until the afternoon. In the autumn and winter Dorian would lose all contact with the light. He opened a wardrobe and then a second one, and the sheer volume of dazzling shirts, jackets and suits had him catch his breath. And there were the sequinned gowns Dorian reserved for drag, and on nights when he made up he would spend hours applying a dark-green mascara or shaping his lipstick bow with a red lip pencil. The collection, like that of all good clothes, looked as though a painter had instructed a couturier.

In his despondency Harry took out a black sequinned jacket lined with gold silk, to be worn with gold Turkish trousers. It was one of Dorian's many ostentatious ensembles. He flung it on the bed as the exotic skin of the mutant he had resolved to leave. He was determined that these would be his final hours in the apartment. He sat on the bed and reviewed his catastrophic past with Dorian. All the symbols of their nocturnal excesses were hidden in this apartment, but he, Harry, had always retained a remove from Dorian's immersion in depradation and commitment to occult study. The occult and alchemical works that Dorian consumed, the works of John Dee and Thomas Vaughan, lives of Gilles de Rais, the Marquis de Sade's scatological novels, the works of Eliphas Levi and J.K. Huysmans, and a whole compendium of privately printed erotica. And there were the ritualistic accoutrements to Dorian's reading; the perfumes, ceremonial robes and sex toys that made up his secret life. Dorian had grown to be a hierophant of the bizarre.

Harry wanted to be free of the whole suffocating system. His attraction to Dorian had closed down his capacity to live. He was wasted. He had gravitated to the night side of life for so long that he was cut off from normal society. The night coated him like a skin. It was on him like a dark-blue pigment. He would leave Paris, go in retreat to a private clinic and from there re-establish contact with his wife. It would be a period of preparation for an imagined rehabilitation. He felt the need to tell his story somehow, but who would believe him, and was there anyone suited to hearing his narrative of a journey through the underworld? His hands trembled. He was in danger of becoming a parody of Dorian rather than a self-expressive individual. And almost nothing in the apartment was his. A few clothes, for he mostly wore Dorian's, a shelf of novels, items of jewellery. He would travel light. He decided he would check into the Ritz, and then formulate his plans from there. He had lived for so long in somebody else's shadow that he had come to neglect himself. He needed the oxygen of convivial company and a return to London life.

He filled a green leather valise with clothes, and looked at the room a long time. The sacrificial victim would return to his double night at any time. He would suspect that Harry was out later than he had been and collapse into bed. When he discovered a day or two later that Harry wasn't simply taking refuge in a hedonistic relationship, the hunt would be on. He was carrying Dorian's secret as well as his own. Harry knew there was a reason that neither should ever be told.

He slammed the door, walked out to the street, looked back a last time and disappeared into a cab. It was still raining, but there were blue splashes in the sky rather like the spaces in his mind which permitted him to hope. He was too tired to keep awake, and his last visual caption in the cab before he blacked out was the memory of a young girl crossing the street. She was dressed in a black coat and had a red scarf in her hair. She was reading a letter, and as she averted her head towards the cab, Harry knew it was a love-letter. She was running down the street to meet the new day, elated with a wild, youthful joy.

Chapter 2

DORIAN came to in the late afternoon. He lay half awake in the cobalt bedroom, situating himself, reconnecting with consciousness and expecting to hear Harry busy about the apartment. He knew from its stillness that the apartment was empty and surmised that Harry must have characteristically delayed a luncheon rendezvous. He was exhausted. The momentous whipping he had received the previous night was the consummation of his extreme sexual fantasies. He had won the leather crown and would be recognised as an S & M divinity to his nocturnal lodge. He knew the ordeal risked death, but he had carried it through with a shamanic sense of dissociation from acts of self-dismemberment. And in going beyond himself, in shifting his psychic boundaries, he had hoped to elude his former self and convert to a Dorian free of the past. He was obsessed by the idea of psychological perspective and of outdistancing himself, almost like someone literally wanting to get away from the past by driving a car at burn-out speed towards the future. He had spent so much time looking at the oneiric fantasies expressed through his dream states, in the hope of subverting his responsibility for the crimes he knew himself to have committed. He had succeeded for whole weeks in satisfying himself that he could achieve a state of voluntary suggestion conducive to convincing himself that his murders were the product of dreams, night statements with which he identified so closely that he had come to adopt their reality. And by further altering his states of consciousness through the use of drugs, he had found release through multiple surrogate identities. He was no longer always identifiable to himself. He could go out on a long lead and be somebody else.

He sat up in bed. His two pet snakes, Sodom and Gomorrah, were dormant in their miniature vivarium. Their compact pythonic energies were capable of extending across the universe with one telescoped jab of a wedged head. He had surrounded himself with a cultivated menagerie of reptiles and stuffed animals. A tiger and a leopard stared at each other across opposite sides of the bedroom. He had contrived to give the leopard emeralds for eyes and the tiger rubies. There were jackals' heads, hyenas'. In his secret library there were mannequins modelled on the extraterrestrials he imagined inhabited a parallel dimension. And there were also his ideally proportioned human bodies. A doll made to resemble a Thai boy, diamond and sapphire chips for toes, the fingernails painted black, and a girl with a corresponding figure, both of which were kept to gratify his eye for aesthetic pleasure.

He listened again and, certain the apartment was empty, crawled out of bed feeling every muscle resist the effort. He filled a tumbler with whisky, his nerves crowding for the shot, and relapsed into a chair. He was angry that Harry was not there to assist, but glad also that he was not called on to explain his acute suffering. He wished he was a thousand miles from nowhere, and then he wished he was situated again in the unsparing pain he had suffered. That too was a refuge from all he could not face, and a going beyond it. Pain was a trajectory to re-creating himself. If he could stay in the intense moment when he was jolted into another realisation of being, that blinding wall of volatile shock transmitted to his body, he would be free. It was this attempted masochistic apotheosisation that drove him back again and again to the underworld, and always with the expectation that he would wake up the next day as somebody else.

Dorian applied perfume from a stoppered Guerlain bottle, and poured out a generous shot of whisky. These days he needed it to right himself. He experienced that little balancing check-point of alignment with his natural functions after his second tumbler of whisky. He was coming alive, making a snapshot of the day around him and attempting to configure plans for the night ahead. He felt as though the preceding night had lasted a lifetime. He saw it as a square black space, a frame in which he had hung suspended by chains.

Harry simply was not around. Dorian went into the drawing-room, and deliberated over whether to draw the curtains. It would be dark already. If the couple in the opposite apartment materialised, it would not be until later. There was no note, nothing from Harry, and Dorian felt a pervasive sense of disquiet. He felt as though something had been irretrievably displaced in his mind. He had lost touch with the instrument controlling his existence. Harry rarely extended his independence without qualifying his movements and company, for to do so would express a code of disloyalty in the relationship which neither was willing to admit. Dorian was too distracted to busy himself with arranging the profuse volume of heady roses that proliferated throughout the room. Their scent was like a solid wall. In his purple silk pyjamas, a tumbler of whisky in one hand, and a copy of Huysmans's *À Rebours* under the other arm, he felt exposed to the intolerability of being. What sustained him was the letter he had received from Oscar Wilde with the promise that, after his release from gaol, he would come and visit him in Paris. Dorian's sympathy with Wilde's predicament, and his penalisation by a judge for sexual corruption with a coterie of boys, had led the equally bizarre Dorian to correspond with Wilde, whose fine sensibility had been savaged by the unmitigating severity of prison. Wilde's imprisonment had instigated a homosexual Diaspora, the whole tenuously balanced social infrastructure had collapsed, sending men running out into the night and towards the far corners of the globe. It was not, Dorian reflected, Wilde who had been imprisoned, it was freedom itself that had been handcuffed and led into a cell. What had replaced it was fear, a grizzled skull with red eyes and an Empire flag unrolling from its lolling tongue. Dorian resented all forms of social conformity, and saw the latter dictate as the endemic menace that denied individuation. Afraid to expand, the individual contracted and conformed to the social preconceptions expected of him. He had risked defying every moral convention, but in his own mind he would die free.

Dorian reread Wilde's letter written on prison notepaper from Reading Gaol, and empathised deeply with the compassion displayed by its author. It seemed Oscar had discovered through suffering a degree of forgiveness for everyone. He had denied his enemies the pleasure of seeing him suffer by removing himself from pain. Dorian recognised in Wilde a redemptive faculty, a light that shone too brightly for the punitive measures calculated to break him. Dorian had resolved that he would help Wilde on his release from prison. He would make money available to him, and the refuge of an apartment if he needed it. Dorian looked forward to discussing notions of good and evil with Wilde, and he felt an immediate confraternity with a man who was also involved in a journey through the transformative underworld. Experiential truths would crystallise from their long immersion in the night. Dorian, who was looking for ways to go beyond himself and create a self distinct from the past, hoped that Wilde would point him in that direction. There would be a new day in which an appointed species would come out of hiding. Gold would be discovered in the streets, the seven days of the week would troop into town, each wearing a different-coloured dress, and resign the livid banners on which their names were written. There would be a cortège taking death to the grave, burying it in a crater over which ten oak forests would be planted, death's giant black feathers spreading across the universe, breaking through the massive foliage. There would be a death of ideologies. Public fountains would pour with hallucinogens. Eagles would whip the air with their red feathers. Silver shoes would waterfall out of a travelling cloud. And the new species would be silver. Dorian had already seen them. He wanted to live in a world that legitimised the marvellous. And had he not found in Wilde's *The Picture of Dorian Gray* the expectation of a world radically transformed in the night, so that the sleeper on waking would be liberated from his past? It was this passage in Wilde's novel that had first won his admiration and attention. It was a literature that transcended its social fabric which thrilled Dorian with its impulsive mania to imagine the impossible. He had withdrawn into a long contemplation of the night in order to realise this vision. In the still conspiratorial dark, waiting out the hour before dawn, hoping that dawn would arrive as a blue angel on the cupola, anything and everything could still happen. The big breakthrough was always imminent. Dorian had hoped in that way he would never grow old. Cellular and physiological decay would be reversed. Red tigers would chase politicians out of town. The new day would arrive. The past would appear like a snapshot bleached out by sunlight.

He was still expectant of hearing Harry's key turn in the lock. He hallucinated the latter calling out to him from the hall, 'Dorian, I'm back.' And despise Harry as he did for carrying his secret, he needed him. Life without him would be like being marooned at the end of the world. He knew he could never again begin to retell his story. There was something so intractable about personal narrative that it could be committed only once, and after that it became a series of variations on a theme. Any number of untruths constellated around a quasar hidden in the unconscious.

Dorian was starting to panic. He drew the curtains, but the windows in the opposite apartment were blank. The couple were not at home, and there was no external distraction to diminish his tension. The night that had gone and the one to come were building to a sonic roar in his head. The faces at which he had snatched, fragmented facial plane by plane, were staring him out. The ones he had used, the clandestine contacts, the impossible inventory of unassimilated needs. He had broken and been broken. Harry was an additional casualty sucked into that vortex of flotsam. And Dorian reflected on how he needed to keep him there, no matter the pain it caused him to see another ruined. Sometimes he imagined he was treading on snakes when he went out into the night. He could feel the recoil beneath his feet, the head alert to strike. And without having met Oscar, and with only the idea of the man as reviled criminal and sexual outlaw, he found himself conferring with him on an inner plane, and looking for the support that his own unconscious refused to give him. Already in Harry's brief absence he had taken to creating a consolatory inner voice, and one he associated with Wilde, that would vindicate areas in which he located the wound.

Dorian could find no respite in anything. He thought of lighting a joint, or of sitting quietly with his hookah, a copy of *Les Fleurs du Mal* open in front of him. He would dress for the night, but he was anxious not to go out before Harry had returned. He was due to meet Nadja, the drag pimp who sold him drugs, and who lived off the Rue de Bercy. He had met Nadja at the bottom of an alley, in August, on one of his rare explorations of the city by daylight. He had been standing at the entrance to a door, his hair cut short and dyed the white of the tight sheath he was wearing. Dorian had known instantly that this was a man, the red lipstick gash and black saucer-shaped eyes serving as livid over-pronouncements of gender transfer. Nadja manifested no show of being extraordinary. He was perfectly normal in his world, and he cared nothing for the rest. He made money out of his difference. He was defiant, confident and bitchily self-assertive. He had looked at Dorian in a way that was acquisitively suggestive, and as though his invincible demeanour could be cracked like a safe. Dorian had wondered whether to move on without extending the contact, but he had accepted Nadja's invitation to come up to his loft and smoke. Nadja's feminine bedroom boasted a display of sailors' hats and uniforms picked up from clients, and kept as fetish trophies. There was a mattress on the floor surrounded by bright cushions, and pictures of actresses and glamour queens tacked to the wall. The room emanated low life, and Dorian had found himself compelled to fit in with Nadja's manipulative ways of forcing him reluctantly to divulge aspects of his personal life.

Dorian threw his mind back to their regular meetings. What he wanted from Nadja were the drugs that would help him forget. But he also liked playing with danger. He knew that Nadja drew him over the safety mark. He had begun by confiding small things, and in the process feared the big truths would follow. It was a dangerous game. He had taken to lighting fires in the corners and then attempting to blow them out. He knew intuitively that Nadja had something on him. Somewhere in the night, voiced in a smoky bar, his secret was out. He half expected the first hints of blackmail to come, each time they met. And he knew it would begin with one of Nadja's off-centre, thin-lipped, tomato-red smiles. Nadja would pin him with small allusions, play him line, let him go out on the illusion that he was still free, then work towards one unflinching truth after the other. He knew it in his mind, and he dreaded the reality.

Dorian had let the matter of his portrait go unattended. He had fled with it at the time of murdering his half-brother, and he had not dared look at the painting again, fearing its recriminations would once again be repeated on his face. By freeing himself of the obsession, he had lived with less specific anxiety of being found out. He rarely considered his age, his good looks had proved a permanent feature in life, and he continued to live as he had always done, with a racy, immediate bite at the moment. If he feared age and cellular degeneration it was because he was fixed in the temporal. His good looks were associated with stepping into awareness in a way that others never forgot. But it occurred to him that Nadja alone refused to acknowledge his physical beauty and saw through to the deception involved in his counterfeit youth. Dorian knew the risk he would be entertaining in a matter of hours. What he fought against was ever realising limitations. Once you accepted the latter, youth was a thing of the past.

He occupied himself with opening his specially bound copy of Baudelaire's *Les Fleurs du Mal*. He had had the book made up for him in London, and bound in black silk from an item of Jeanne Duval's lingerie, or so the slip had been described in the auctioneer's catalogue. He had been an obsessive collector of weird memorabilia, and his fingers delighted in sensually appraising this item. Baudelaire's fingers must also have lived on the fabric in its tight adherence to his mistress's curves. It was the poet's inveterate concern with age and time that appealed to Dorian. Baudelaire's lyric voice transcended existential despair. This man who shaved his skull like a convict, manicured his nails like a diva, and who pursued at a distance the Parisian hookers whom he would never dare approach, had earned for himself the name of Paris prowler. The poet had grown to be a wolf in the twilight. That he had studiously pursued an asexual policy towards the women in his life, contrasted with the sensuality of his work. Dorian took comfort in Baudelaire's pathology. The poet's expression of being irretrievably lost to the shadow was like the howl of a wolf in stony hills. Baudelaire had injected toxins into lyric blood. The viral content of his work would elude the antibodies massing to resist it. In his mind Dorian could see Baudelaire dressed in black, sitting alone in a restaurant, sipping a glass of Nuits-Saint-Georges, his contempt and arrogance pushing him out to the edge of the world. This poet who had called for the return of capital punishment would have operated the killing machine with white-gloved fingers.

Dorian lost himself momentarily in Baudelaire's satanic invocations. *Les Fleurs du Mal*, together with Huysmans's *À Rebours*, were his constant points of reference. They had come to provide an inner geography to his unconscious. Dorian's own exile had begun a long time ago. He had never fitted into any situation, and the extravagant wealth made available to him had allowed him to deepen his sense of isolation. He had lost touch with his past: there had been some psychic breakage, and when it did intrude it was through the free association of dreams rather than a chronology alerting him to retrospective evaluation. In London, sitting behind the olive satin curtains drawn over the three tall windows in his bedroom, he had begun the process of displacement. It was as though he had died but could claim no evidence for being dead. He had got so far wide of instinctual human functioning and all the emotional interconnectives that bring people together that his life had become a defiant subversion of the natural. If he was dead, the state was not fully realised. It was as if he were standing at the entrance to a corridor and had still to find the code to explore its interior. Wasn't every state, he considered, purely experiential? You found yourself in it, and you followed it through. The actual difference between life and death might be only the quality of not knowing one from the other. Dorian liked to think long on these subjects. He had confused himself over the issue of identity until he no longer knew anything with clarity. He had attempted to confront no one as himself, but there had always been someone there to own to no one. Even mixtures of cocaine and heroin had still left him with a subliminal sense of identity. Some sort of consciousness was always there like a light in the back of his head.

Dorian began to dress with the indecisiveness of a man who would like to go through six costume changes an hour. He flung a slew of rain-forest-coloured garments on the bed. Silk shirts and sequinned jackets contended for attention. He settled for mauve and black – mauve shirt worn with a black velvet suit. He would combine the fashionable with his adopted air of gravity. Whatever authority he retained over Nadja he would continue to press home by way of maintaining an invincible aura of mystique. Dorian's discomfort in Nadja's company was not only his expectation of being found out, but his sense of continued apprehension at Nadja's allusions to blackmailing friends who lived at the other end of the night. 'There's nobody here, but there's somebody.' He kept remembering a line of Rimbaud's which Verlaine had pointed out to him at Le Procope. He felt that sort of indefinable presence in his meetings with Nadja. There was somebody else there, who was arguably his double waiting to reproach him for the crimes he attempted to conceal. And how would it differ, he wondered, if he confessed the buried contents of his life? If he dug the black stuff out of his nerves, would he have disowned it? In his own mind he had committed his actions to disinformation. He felt he had not only prevented external inquiry, but that he too would never find a way to recollect the truth. He was guilty of everything and nothing.

Dorian resigned himself to the fact that he would have to go out before Harry's return. He needed drugs from Nadja and the adrenalin fix which exploring the night invariably gave him. There was the possibility of encountering the marvellous – the new day burning in the night as a big red ballroom splashed with gold stars. If Dorian had encountered angels in life, he had attributed their qualities to androgynes, transvestites, transexuals, the whole order of mutants and gender-benders who materialised in the night. It was the attempted physiological transformation that found a deep resonance in his psyche. He had searched for fallen angels in every alley. A man looking like a girl, and coming at him with a livid red lipstick gash, was for him a form of self-created divinity. He would be compelled to follow and in that way he had learnt of the bars, cafés, nightclubs and resorts where an alternative culture pursued its ends. The night angels were known to each other, their competitive underworld coterie disappearing at sunrise.

Dorian found consolation in the night. It was like living on borrowed or extended time. He had struck an orphic pact with the Dionysian elements of the unconscious. Psychopathology gravitated to the midnight sun. He had seen a château materialise on waste-land, its windows blazing with light; he had watched a black angel fly from one roof ledge to another. He had seen the dead sitting outside cafés boarded up for the night, and he had encountered a drag queen leading fifty chihuahuas, each with a sparkling *diamanté* collar, across a moonlit square. The night was as full of surprises as the trillions of stars in the galaxies. Dorian had seen a naked woman sitting astride a statue in the Luxembourg Gardens, her hips rotating rhythmically as she built to a suitable climax. He had stood back against a wall as four men dressed in leather, and supporting on their shoulders a girl, who carried an altar candle, hurried towards the river, singing. He had followed and watched them set fire to a barge. The girl had stripped and jumped naked into the river, still supporting her candle. And there had been times at night when the rain had instated a crystal wall. It had built to a constantly collapsing glass palace. Dorian had stood open-handed under the elemental illusion, his palms drumming with flashpoints. He had felt connected to the whole brilliant sky.

He slipped out of the apartment into a blue-black October night. Something kept on clicking in his mind, and he knew it was association with loss. Harry must have cleared out. He felt it in his abdomen like a bass chord. There was suddenly nobody in his life. There was this big drop down the quarry-face to a deep pool. He found a cab and headed over to a maze of alleys off the Rue de Bercy. It was a part of his secrecy that he would never have a cab drop him at his destination. Instead, he preferred to linger in the alleys, and leave himself open to chance meetings before calling at Nadja's place.

The night was high and blue and cold. There were a few transvestites standing against doorways, their dresses tight on the skin like pigment on canvas. One was mouthing smoke into the air, one had placed a white tulip in the pronounced V of a black dress. Dorian took them in like someone hoping for redemption in the curious. There was a black one in a scarlet dress with the back cut out. His earrings flashed like rainstorms. A tall transvestite, in a short white skirt, fitted a finger inside a taut suspender-strap as Dorian moved out of shadow and into the light. He had come to recognise faces in his night patrol, an itinerary that he had differed every night in order to make his curiosity appear less familiar. He was frightened he would be taken for a decoy or a prowler. The transvestites all smiled at him. He felt isolated by his search for the impossible. He was looking for an angel who would also fulfil his sexual fantasies, a leopard-spotted body charged by the supra-real.

He took a last turn down the alley, and headed towards Nadja's place. The night was turning cold. The sky was brilliant with its overload of stars. It was Harry's image which pushed too close into his consciousness. There was something wrong, and his mind accelerated the possibilities of his lover being injured, the victim of a street-gang, or amnesiac in a park, or dead, calling out from a paranormal dimension and not being heard. He saw their past together as a series of random flashbacks. Pain crowded into his mind, and alternated with its opposite, the relief that he was no longer constrained by an intensely discomforting relationship. Dorian took momentary refuge in the belief that if Harry was dead, then at least he would be silent, no matter how telepathically he buzzed him. And then he turned on a knife of jealousy, imagining Harry won over by a new love, or returned to his wife. He walked with his mind distracted by conflicting possibilities.

Nadja's window up on the top floor of an eighteenth-century house had its usual red light showing through the drawn blinds. The room was like a perverse sanctuary, a drug den full of mats and photographs of idols. Dorian's mind travelled back to his time in London and the little Florentine table that had stood beside his bed, and the purple satin coverlet embroidered with gold he had kept drawn over his portrait in a secret room. His excursions into low life near Blue Gate Fields had been the start of his fascination with descent. Harry had stood there pointing the way, but had never accompanied him into the tunnel. Only much later, when it was Dorian who showed the way, had Harry followed, a symbiotic accomplice claiming to be victim.

Dorian found a note on the door telling him to go up and wait, Nadja would be back in five minutes. The communal stair had wooden boards that looked as though they were wine stained. There was a smell of incense caught up on the air. When he got to the top, Nadja's door was off the latch. Dorian walked in and sat down on black and red cushions, and watched a thin column of incense snake from a cone burning in a saucer. Nadja's only possessions were clothes and glam photographs. Sailors' caps were hung on nails over the bed. Dorian acclimatised himself to the room, and felt the pockets of tension distributed from his throat to the abdomen. He sat waiting on his life and death. It was the expectation of the latter that heightened the excitement he experienced in the sexual chase. He had taken to living in the moment so intensely that time had come to assume tangible proportions. He held on to its tail even if the scales came off in his hands and he admitted defeat. Those scales glinted green and gold like a grass snake before evaporating on his fingertips. Dorian picked up on the tense atmospherics. There was a half-smoked joint in the ashtray. He lit it and inhaled, his nerves coming on, and sat legs crossed, one hand placed over the other, as was his way. The night outside was solid. There was little street noise, just the thrum of traffic which had about it the unreality of a sound-track.

He sat waiting, and when he heard footsteps down in the street, clicking a fast pace, he knew it was Nadja returning. He heard his heels negotiating the stairs. There was a determination to his steps at all times, which spelt out resolution. His femininity was only the exterior of a defiant masculine orientation.

Dorian dragged deeply on the joint. Nadja's handcuffs were on the bed, and his eye caught the dull glint of the fastenings. Somewhere in the sky he thought he heard thunder, the reverberation buried in a dense cloud wall like a drum being played under water. There must have been a storm building, or else the reverberation was in his head. He tensed as Nadja came into the room, his mouth made up like a poppy with a wide horizontal gash. He was wearing a little black outfit, probably stolen from the Worth collection, and he had taken off his shoes and was carrying them in his hands like two art objects. Nadja closed the door and locked it, a procedure he had never done before. He went straight over to the bed and, throwing himself back on it, picked up the handcuffs. Dorian felt partly relieved that the invitation was sexual, but his sense of disquiet would not disperse.

'Come over here, love,' Nadja teased. 'I like you in handcuffs. I know what you want, don't I?'

Dorian responded. His capacity for masochism was unlimited. And it was Nadja's hold on him. He took off his black velvet jacket and went over to the bed. He knew there was something wrong, but an electric stimulus shot through his nerves. Nadja formally fitted the right and then the left fastening in position, and snapped the mechanism shut. Dorian felt a big jab of adrenalin shoot through his heart.

'I've got you now, sugar,' Nadja cajoled, and then with a voice radically changed in tone, 'I've got you, and I've waited a long time for this.' He lifted Dorian's face up to his and coldly sneered, 'I know your story. I've been piecing it together bit by bit. You're red hot with crime, aren't you?' He pushed Dorian away, who sat passively facing inner chaos.

'I know who you are,' Nadja continued. 'You're Dorian Gray, presumed dead by the British police. Your name is linked to the disappearance of an artist called Basil Hallward. Remember Basil, Dorian?'

Dorian was being jerked into an insufferable awareness of his past. He tasted something in his throat which could have been ashes or blood. It was like the smell of streets after rain. He half expected Nadja to claim that he had informed the police, but then the clearer awareness of blackmail jumped into his head. He was waiting for it to come through the invidiously subtle spectrum by which words slowly revealed a person's inner contents. Nadja was suddenly in a position of omnivorous power. He bit his tomato-coloured bottom lip, and his bumped-up eyes walked into Dorian's.

'I probably know things about you that you've forgotten,' he said, with the calculated detachment of someone who had played over the scene endlessly in his mind. The rehearsals showed in Nadja's neutrality, the objectivity with which he refused to express emotion or rush his statement.

Dorian cold-sweated at the power-field from which Nadja was directing words.

'I've got you detail by detail in here,' Nadja resumed, running a finger from his forehead down to his abdomen. 'And I've waited a long time for this, darling.'

Dorian felt he had been dropped into the night river. He was struggling with a weight that swallowed him. The water was inside his nostrils.

'I could run you in,' Nadja continued. 'But that's largely up to you. You're ready for sex, aren't you?' Nadja sneered. 'I could let you go out to the street in handcuffs like an escaped criminal, but you wouldn't be of use to me like that.'

'What is it you want?' Dorian found himself saying, aware as he was speaking of the uselessness of his words.

'I want to tell you your own story,' Nadja replied with consummate irony. 'As I said, you may have forgotten your past. You may need me to remind yourself of things that you wouldn't wish others to know. I have my sources. Nadja's friends know everything. You forget, Dorian, that transvestites live a dual life. We are men who gossip like women. We hear things that usually only women hear. You should keep out of our affairs.'

'Why do you think I'm Dorian Gray?' Dorian inquired, again playing for time.

'For the reason that you can't bear the story I'm about to tell you,' Nadja delivered with supreme irony. 'You thought your secret was the one which would never get out,' said Nadja.

41

'Everyone thinks that. But secrets, honey, blow about on the wind for a long time. Some people might say for ever. And yours got blown to my feet. You murdered Basil Hallward by repeatedly stabbing him with a knife behind the ear. And then you found crime to meet your ends came easy. You experienced no remorse, so you wanted to try it again. But you see, Hallward was known to us, he was a regular at La Rose Noire, a club in Montmartre. He was due to stay with a friend of mine at the time of his disappearance. I knew, we knew, he hadn't gone missing in Paris. Basil wasn't like that. The fact is, you had his body dissolved by an obliging friend who later committed suicide.'

'This is your story,' Dorian said, dispassionately, determined to dissociate himself from the subject under discussion. 'It's not mine. Now release me from these handcuffs.'

'I'm not letting you go,' said Nadja. 'You are handcuffed to remind yourself that you are a criminal. I am going to carry on with the rest of your story. You didn't stop with Basil, somebody knew you'd killed him, and that was your illegitimate brother. You see, Basil was not only generous, but he dipped deep into the night side of life. He pursued rent. Jim, the brother you so readily spat out of your life, was part of Hallward's circle. He schemed. He knew you were responsible for the murder, and he pressed you for money. You had to eliminate him, and make it look like it was you who had died.'

Dorian had never before heard so much that he did not wish to hear. He could taste river water in his throat.

'You placed your rings on his fingers after you'd killed him. There was enough of a physical resemblance for the body to pass as yours. And anyhow, society didn't need an excuse to have you out of the way. Nobody wanted to mention your name. The police never opened an inquiry. You were officially buried without an inquest. It took place on a rainy winter's day at Highgate Cemetery. Your family denied your burial in their vault. And I was unnaturally interested in your story. All of my life I've been fascinated by outlaws, criminals, the mad. You think I am street trash, but that's your mistake. It's not lack of education that makes me different, it's my dislike of convention. You confused the two, and you are going to pay for it for the rest of your life.'

Dorian felt time stand still. There was suddenly too much of it. It was like stepping off momentum into a waste-land that had materialised between two busy streets. He felt as though his nervous impulses had been demagnetised. He was completely vulnerable to his inquisitor. And Nadja was without let-up.

'And so I put your story together. I knew you had to emerge from hiding and that you'd go back to the world which you knew. That's the problem. We never change. If you had looked to disappear you would have changed your contacts. You simply exchanged one place for another. That's why people get caught. You and Harry. You were too conspicuous in the night. You imagined you were invisible, but every club got to know of you. By denying yourself a day life, you stood out in the night. Even trash like me live in the day. You became one of the night people. There was something wrong. Word was out. You don't know how many barmen watched you, how many rent-boys observed your guilt. Your tips were always too large, and your needs too demanding. Even our world has limitations. And because you observed none, your guilt stood out.'

Dorian contracted into an inner freeze. He thought his heart had stopped; there was no bass chord sequence in his diaphragm.

'And bit by bit I tracked you. We're a small world. And your habit made you sink deep into it. The man was watching you. A man. The man. I could give you a street map of the places you visit in Paris. It was as if you had red paint under the soles of your shoes. You left a trail, Mr Gray.'

'What are you going to do with me?' Dorian asked. 'What do you want of me? Can't you take these things off?'

'You're going to sweat it out, honey,' Nadja drawled, turning up the malevolence in his eyes so that they were all black pupil. 'Men like you live out of time. Do your victims return, asking for more of the life you took from them? I suppose you need to kill Harry and now me, and whoever else has access to your past. I'll trade my secret for money. But big money, Mr Gray. I deserve a more comfortable life-style, don't you think?

Glamour needs its corresponding luxuries. I'm not just rent. I'm a WOMAN.'

Dorian bit hard on his lip. Money comprised his protective security. He had used it as a paper castle. To lose it would be to expose himself to every form of threat. He could smell, taste, hear, see and feel his fear. It was insupportable, like a ship sitting in his chest.

'How much do you want, and who have you told?' he heard himself saying, as though his voice had acquired an autonomy independent of breath. Somebody else was speaking for him.

'I'll tell you that when I've checked your accounts,' said Nadja. 'We'll begin in the region of quarter of what they represent and move up from there. My needs are unlimited.'

Dorian had the image of Nadja making a telescopic ladder out of paper money, all the way to the stars. Money that was tainted, splashed with a patina of the black arts.

'What's out is out,' Nadja continued. 'It's like currency in our world. Everyone's got something on somebody. We have got big things on you. When you're that far gone, you need a compensatory balance. And with you that means money. You'll pay for your freedom, or else.'

'What does that mean?' said Dorian.

'You wait and find out. It will be your next surprise,' said Nadja, pushing his lower lip up into a pout. 'I want the money within a week. And don't try to get away, Mr Gray. You'll be watched. The man will be following you. Like I told you. A Man. The Man. And in case you're wondering, Harry's gone. He left from the Gare du Nord this morning. You see, I have eyes and ears everywhere in every city. Eyes stuck to your back. And now that you've lost your witness, you have me.'

Dorian felt his life collapse on him like a building landsliding over the edge of a cliff. His emotional infrastructure had been fissured. He imagined Harry at the alienating terminal, his perfect clothes and hauteur having him stand out in the crowd, the decision to leave written on his face, the platform smelling of a tear-splashed future. Jerky, kinetic sequences flashed across his mind. The possibilities, the impossibilities, the refusal to accept Harry's departure as a truth, the belief that it was all a

fiction and that Harry was really back at home waiting for him.
'I've nothing on Harry,' said Nadja. 'He's gay, but he wants
the compensation of a wife. Men like that are in search of crazy
sensation. They oscillate in their preferences. Now a woman,
now a man. I don't take them seriously. It's you and I who are
the real things. . . . I'd like to send you out to the street in
handcuffs, but it doesn't serve my purpose to draw attention to
you yet. It would make it too easy for the law. You would have
arrested yourself.'

Nadja produced a key. He held it up with a faggotish, deistic
omnipotence. He suspended it in front of Dorian's eyes. All of
the suppressed malevolence of the man living out of context as
a woman was realised in that gesture. The gender imbalance
created a freakish perversity. Fuelled by the conflict within himself, his mood was dominated by an exhibitionistic megaloma-
nia. He stood back from Dorian like a stripper. He ran a hand
over the contour of his hips and thighs. He was a transvestite
diva. Acting out power to a criminalised victim increased his
sense of parodic invention. Dorian found himself confronted by
a maniacal dervish. Nadja prolonged the intensification of his
female characteristics. His red fingernails were thrown into a
flamenco dance. When he came back to himself he presented
the key and used it. Left hand and right hand, Dorian was free
of the biting metal constriction. His wrists and his mind breathed.
His inner turbulence was like an earthquake flaw tearing across
a parched continent. Everywhere he looked strata were breaking up, huge cracks were making inroads into the landscape.
His one immediate consolation was the idea of travel. He would
get away from Paris. He would forget Harry, his past, and start
again somewhere else. Redemption would come with the idea
of reinventing himself.

Dorian went back to a street that had radically changed. Nadja's
mark was burnt into his nerves. The night was a blue curve,
the spiral arm of the galaxy receding to deep space, glitter along
its twisted spine.

Dorian dispensed with the idea of immediately returning to
his apartment. He needed to be around people in order to
think, but instinctual panic told him to keep clear of the network.

He had to decide whether to stay or go, and even if he did pay Nadja off, he would have to leave Paris instantly. He kept playing over in his mind what had initially attracted him to Nadja. He saw him again white-haired and in a white dress, standing outside an open door in the late afternoon. But it had not begun there, he was sure of that now. Nadja must have been in so many of the bars and clubs he had visited. His eye would have monitored Dorian's contacts and pick-ups. And he must have gone to Harry. The possibility of the latter's connivance injected rage into Dorian's system. He was aware that he could trust no one and nothing. He sat in a cab speeding across the city – via Place d'Italie, the streets lit by blue and red neons – and he realised that everyone was known, no matter how anonymously they lived. There was nothing which could be completely buried inside or out. Somebody knew and that person was yourself.

Dorian had the cab-driver take him to Montmartre. He walked through the streets, skipping traffic, distracted, and occasionally stopping to look in shop windows. He knew of a mixed club on the corner of Rue de Richelieu. There was a pink neon cat outside as the club's sign. Dorian needed alcohol to fire his shot nerves. The girl who let him into the club was dressed as a black velvet cat. Eye-liner, green lenses, thigh boots, and the second skin afforded by her jumpsuit all contrived to enhance her sensual feline characteristics.

Dorian was taken downstairs to the interior of an exclusive club. The table-lamps were pink, and there was an arrangement of black roses at each table. The bar was heart-shaped, and a Negro wearing stalactital drop-earrings was in the process of mixing a cocktail. The mirror behind him was studded with paste jewels, and on its surface someone had placed the imprint of red lips. There was a photograph above the mirror of someone Dorian recognised, and on closer observation he could see it was signed *Oscar Wilde*. His long hair parted in the middle was concealed beneath an angled wide-brimmed hat. A cloak complemented the outfit. The man had affected the stylised aestheticism of the artist of his period.

When the barman saw Dorian's interest in the photograph, he said, 'You know him. He's started coming here again. He's out, and living here in Paris. He's a famous writer, isn't he? And there was that scandal. Goes under the name of Sebastian Melmoth now. But we call him Oscar.'

Dorian experienced an immediate emotive lift. The possibility that he would at last meet Oscar Wilde hit a shift of mood in him. He would extend his time in Paris to allow for the meeting, no matter his fear of Nadja. Meeting Wilde carried with it the idea of personal redemption. Dorian needed to hold a hand that had emerged from the night carrying a rose. He was fixated by the photograph. He ordered a drink and returned to his table. If he was being watched, if the omniscient eye was travelling over the back of his head, brushing his shoulders, returning again to explore a facial plane in profile, then he was for a moment sure in the affirmative knowledge that he could go on. He relaxed inside the moment. The barman winked at him with a cutie eye. He felt centred, no matter his life was being tapped and his nerves were shredded. He could come back here until he encountered Oscar. Only then would he surrender himself to the endless night.

Chapter 3

DORIAN made the same journey the following night to Mont-martre. He was still living with the belief that Harry's disap-pearance from his life was a fiction, and that at any moment he would walk back into the apartment and account for his ab-sence with the usual languid witticisms that gave such an indi-vidual tang to his conversation.

He took a cab over to the club, and pursued his usual para-noid habit of having the driver drop him in the street parallel to his intended destination. He expected to see Nadja in every doorway, one hand on his hip, his mouth pursed into a pro-vocative carnation pout. The eye would be tracking him. The man would follow. He had another five days in which to make a decision either to concede to blackmail or to take flight.

When he entered the club, the same Negro barman wearing sparkling drop-earrings was mixing cocktails at the bar. He looked up and gave Dorian a complicitous wink towards a man sitting alone at a table, smoking a cigarette with the eloquence of the gestural motions accompanying speech. A bottle of Veuve Clicquot was cradled in the ice-bucket beside him. He was wearing a dark-blue suit with a pink carnation splashed in the buttonhole. There was a tipped cane angled against the chair beside him, and periodically he would glance up from the book he was reading, his state of dual consciousness switching to stereo chan-nels as he scanned the bar. His body had now become large, unmuscular and neglected. There was a lack of tone to his shoulders, but the vibrant sensitised generosity that informed the man's features suggested the aesthete was concealed inside the coarsening expansive face. A luminous sense of compassion was visible in the manner in which he reflected on his reading. It was then that the suffering showed through, as though he referenced every thought by its opposite. He had at some time plunged into black water and was now suspicious of the clear.

Dorian knew instantly that the man was Oscar Wilde. The Negro barman confirmed his suspicions by a discreet flick of his eyes towards the contradictory photograph, and then he turned to smooch with his blonde assistant, a strawberry forelock curled between his green eyes.

Dorian ordered a champagne cocktail, and conscious of his own arresting physical beauty took himself over towards Wilde's table. He let his red silk tie flop out of his black velvet jacket. His arranged hair had a wind-stormed effect of mussing into his eyes as the epitome of romanticised glamour. Like Wilde he knew that he had acquired an enhanced beauty by the opposition between mental experience and the retainment of an idealised sense of physical beauty. He stood there, willing to risk everything for the redemptive meeting he had anticipated. And suddenly Wilde looked up and said, 'How good of you, my dear friend, everyone cuts me now', and the immediate bitterness of the comment gave way to the inviting warmth of a man whose instinctive defences were barbed repartee. 'You are just as I imagined Dorian Gray,' he said. 'I knew I wouldn't find or see him until after I described him in my book. You see, my idea is right, that art inspires and directs nature. You would never have existed had I not described Dorian. Do sit down, Mr Gray.'

Dorian was impressed by the spontaneity of Wilde's perception. He sat down opposite the fallen icon, his hand reflexively reaching for his glass, and his eyes lowered in deference to Oscar's. He had the idea that for the first time he would find himself in the company of a listener. Wilde was unhurried in his delivery, and evidently lonely. He too was in need of being heard. He was in Dorian's eyes one of the night lost.

'I have lived with the idea of meeting you for a long time,' Dorian said in a subdued voice. 'It's hard to know where to begin, for I have a story, and I believe that you alone are capable of understanding it. I know it is presumptuous to assume this right, but I somehow feel that we are connected. We had to meet.'

Dorian watched Wilde transfer his attention to his glass. It was as if he could see Oscar's mind in the glass, all the neuronal interconnections fizzing with the measured tick of champagne.

Wilde looked up and said, 'But let me, before you begin, tell you of an incident that happened yesterday. From it you can assess my importance or unimportance to you. I was together with a friend passing over the Pont Neuf, and a woman threw herself into the water. A sailor jumped in to rescue her. I could have rescued that woman. But this act was forbidden me. Yes, it is so. It is horrible. I would have seemed to be seeking attention for myself. Heroism would just have made for scandal. Since my trial, heroism and genius are forbidden me. You have heard how I made efforts to enter a monastery. That would have been the best end. But I would have created a scandal. Pity me. And remember, I could have rescued that woman.'

Dorian watched Wilde retreat into reflective subjectivity, his mind opening and closing doors on the past, surprised or agonised by his findings. Dorian could almost hear a metal door reverberate in Wilde's head before he approached his theme, his listener throwing looks at his eyes and restlessly tracking hands.

'When I first wrote to you,' said Dorian, 'it was because your condition provoked compassion and outrage in me. I have always lived against the grain. But there was another reason. A mixed motive. I had the feeling you had created me through your book. That I had stepped out of your mind and committed the crimes you had imagined on the page. And I am going to tell you that it is I who am the criminal. My actions make yours quite inconsequential in terms of criminality. My story should have taken me into the river, rather like the incident you encountered yesterday, only I should have gone under with my secret. Carrying it around is too much. I am fascinated by the way my inner contents separate me from others. That's probably the reason why I continue to live. But at the same time I am known, I am followed. My secrets are out.'

Wilde averted his eyes in the conscious action of bringing his own experience to bear on another's. Dorian could see him mixing the two like paints. A yellow and a green which in turn formed a dark blue.

'Your story involves me in the despair I had anticipated,' Wilde said. 'I am an outlaw. The century will have known two outlaws, Paul Verlaine and me. You may know that in my prosecution, ideas expressed in my novel were used against me. Fiction was made to seem a reality. But if what you tell me is true, then I was clearly convicted of the wrong crime. A patriot put in prison for loving his country loves his country, and a poet in prison for loving boys loves boys. But the issue goes deeper. If you are Dorian Gray, then I ask you to consider if you have really murdered. Are you not identifying with an act which I conceived as a fiction?'

For a moment Dorian relaxed into the illusion that he was deceiving himself. He wished he could suspend belief in his own ineradicable guilt. He would like to have been able to say that he was the victim of empathetic obsession with a fiction. He would like to have walked away from the club secure in the knowledge of a pathology that would be revised. He could see that Wilde was offering him that hope. He looked over at Wilde, who was nervously pouring another drink.

'It's worse than you can conceive,' Dorian continued. 'And to make matters more complicated, I feel I can confess to no one but you. I have been looking for you for ages. I know you need money, and I will pay you to listen to me. If I can tell you my story, it may be possible for me to continue in life.'

Wilde looked up. 'I have discovered,' he said, 'that alcohol taken in sufficient quantity produces all the effects of drunkenness.'

Dorian observed that this was his way of being serious, and continued: 'I suppose, after what you have suffered, nothing can really shock. But I think my story will. To live out what the imagination suggests is shocking to a writer. And that is my fear. If I was in part created by you, then I ask that you hear me out. And I will pay. You deserve money, and you shall have it.'

'Flattery will get you everywhere,' Wilde observed, leaving Dorian to reconnect with his theme.

'Maybe it is all to do with time,' said Dorian, 'and I sometimes wonder how the acts that have occupied only minutes in a lifetime come to eliminate all that went before, and will come after. They become a block in the arteries. I am of course talking about murder, madness, pathological anomalies. There is something obsessively cyclical to these inner patterns which I can't break.'

'There are moments when it takes you like a tiger by the throat,' said Wilde. 'I too so often acted out of compulsion. I went out into the night with an invisible wind at my back. And I ended up doing what I called feasting with panthers, or being hungry for street-boys.'

Dorian watched a tear badge Wilde's eye. It was like a pear-shaped distillation drawn from his inner suffering.

'Time has never proved a reality in my life,' continued Dorian. 'I have forgotten how old I am and I suspect I never knew. I have lived only at night, and in doing so I lost my association with the changing seasons. Time is always blacked out in my life. Drugs, sex and manipulated states of consciousness do the rest. I am not sure that I am not dead and exist in an extra-temporal state. Who would ever know? Because we are only conditioned to one state of consciousness we lack awareness of its contrast. It is you who should be speaking of these things, but perhaps you will permit me to continue. I don't know how I got into this labyrinth, but I am in it – and there appears to be no way out. And if there is a light at the end of the tunnel, it must be smashed. But let me come back on myself. The night. And Basil Hallward, whom I still see in my worst, hallucinated hours. Sometimes he pulls the knife with which I killed him out of his head, swallows it like a trick, walks towards me and shakes my hand. You can imagine that. The incident keeps on repeating itself in filmic variations. And sometimes I go to a ruined house in the city, and go up the stairs and sit on a packing-crate in the sunlight, and he is there. He's sitting with his head hanging down and his hands on his knees, and when he looks up he takes off his head to convince me he is dead.

One day there were spots on the floor. They looked like red paint, but I am convinced they were blood. And you talk of the river and that woman's failed suicide. I often walk on the banks at night, search out warehouses, sit in barges tied up at the quay, and again he is there. He is luminous, as if he is just nerve, but a red wound stands out. He'll wait a time, and then dive into the waters and swim across the divide to the opposite bank. Or he'll turn round and thrust an arm vertical from the water, as though saluting me. I killed this man in the way you imagined. He had too much on me. It was his incorruptibility I couldn't bear. I wanted him to go to death like that. There was too much contrast between us. I came to loathe myself in his company, so I got rid of him.

'In so many cases of murder,' Dorian continued, 'the balance is usually between killing yourself or the other. I was fascinated to know how life changed if you killed. And then I did it again. I didn't kill myself like your Dorian. I killed my lookalike brother because he was attempting to blackmail me, and I got away a second time with my life. I went into hiding. I became too an extension beyond what you had imagined. And in the same way as Basil wouldn't go away afterwards, so my half-brother Jim hallucinated his way back into my consciousness. I see him pushing a hat towards me. Something jumps inside it like a fish, and I know it is his life he is holding. He can't fit it back into himself. He cries at its elusiveness, then redirects his eyes towards me. And on another night he was sitting on the stairs to my apartment obsessively peeling oranges. I could smell the sharp citric tang of the fruit. He had a sack of them, like potatoes, and he was so concentrated on his occupation that he never once looked at me. I realised of course that he was unable to eat the fruit he was peeling. The scent of oranges wouldn't go away from the stair. It is still there today. The concierge has often remarked on it, but can do nothing to eliminate the smell.

'I won't keep you in silence much longer. You have had time enough in enforced confinement, I am sure, to replay your life over and over again. And it goes on. But things have deepened. I am again being pursued. A transvestite called Nadja has clearly been tracking me for years. He seems to have assembled all the pieces, all the writing in the text. If I don't meet a certain payment I will be done. Anyhow, I have to leave Paris either way. It is odd when you discover that someone knows more about you than you do yourself. I feel as though Nadja has got so deep under my skin that he has lived all the apprehensive fear of my life. He has found me out. I needed to see you to tell you these things. I had to have a witness before I decide either to terminate my life or go on. You are the person I have turned to in my mind again and again, the one I imagined would hear me out, hear me to the end. And there is nothing I would take from you other than your ability to listen.'

Dorian felt himself freeze into the isolating silence that succeeds confession. He was aware that he had undergone a dramatic transformation in his listener's eyes. The metamorphic transition would have shocked Wilde deeply, even if his collected exterior showed no register of the impact. He was busy pouring a glass of champagne, and Dorian motioned to the barman to bring over another bottle. Wilde was collecting his thoughts and Dorian could sense them humming into assembled patterns. All the co-ordinative cells were lighting up with associations.

Wilde kept from speaking until the barman brought over the second bottle of champagne. He fastidiously lit a cigarette, sipping at the gold filter, and choreographed his hand with the self-conscious gestures of an inveterate aesthete. When he looked up, he said, 'I will consider your story. The intense energy of creativity has been kicked out of me, but I still have a mind. Death to think of. It shadows me. My life is like a work of art. An artist never starts the same thing twice. You have taken on some of the moral responsibilities that I wrote about but failed to live. You have gone to the end of the night, and I have taken refuge from it in a cell. But involuntarily. I was put away. Life was taken from me. You live in the apprehension of that happening to you. And don't let it happen. You must reinvent yourself again in order to stay free. I once said that I have put only my talent into my work and my genius into my life. Put yours into your life. You have been asked to experience what very few ever do. You carry in your head the psychological associations of two murders. The people who encounter you in the street have no idea of your inner world. They will stop at your physical beauty. I too was blackmailed. It formed the invidious foundation of my trial. Letters that I had bought back had of course been copied. The boys presented at my trial were exempt from prosecution and paid to bring evidence against me. I too found that word about me was all over London. In gaol, I feared insanity. If I hadn't romanticised the ideal of suffering, I would have killed myself rather than undergo the inhumanity of the ordeal. I died in prison. The man who speaks to you now carries my past, but not my future. I am nobody now. And if you wish to remain somebody, get out of the way of your blackmailers and don't look back. All life is a limitation. Escape with yours and continue to expand it.'

Dorian observed how heavily Wilde was drinking. He was clearly trying to dull his alerted nerves, and even the mention of prison brought him close to breaking down. The system had partially destroyed him, and the gap left by two missing front teeth only heightened the emphasis on his social fall. The desperation beneath his composure was that of a hunted animal still suspicious of being set free. Wilde was struggling to locate the aphoristic brilliance of the speech for which he was renowned. He looked like green jelly which hadn't conformed to the mould.

'So you would advise my getting out as soon as possible,' reflected Dorian. 'Should I pay first to get Nadja off my trail? Or just cut and run?'

'Your losses are already so great, why add financial depletion to them?' said Wilde. 'My attempts to buy back letters never helped my case. It only pronounced my fear. And it is not a contracting circle that closes on you. It is an expanding one that gives you the illusion you have broken free, but the circumference touches on more and more people. Men who talk like that are more dangerous than women. They are women with a man's aggression.'

Dorian felt his isolation turn back on him like deep water in a quarry pool risen after rain. His freedom would always be that of the outlaw, self-created and unshareable. He would no longer live in real time but in a fugitive state, one in which his

non-linear progression was subjected to blocked nervous high-
ways. He looked at how Wilde was inhibited by lack of immediacy. He no longer bit the moment but considered it. He had
been displaced from his temporal and social context in life. There
was an apologetic screen between the man and his relation to
the moment, which Wilde attempted to conceal by caustic hu-
mour. By endlessly deconstructing himself he was able to present
a depersonalised subject to his listener. He would have taken
up with anyone, and entered into any tangent of conversation
rather than be alone. There was a sense of solitude built around
him like ice packed into a glass.

'I am prolonging our meeting,' said Dorian, 'because after
that I am without a confidant – except for the impersonal company that money may buy. I fail, you see, to have learnt from
my actions. My psychological evaluation of events is one thing,
but the emotional knowledge derived from them is another. I
have become fascinated by my shadow. What I have experienced has obsessively replayed itself in so many variations that I
have come to see how an action is translated into any number
of imaginative re-creations. Does this also make me capable of
committing those actions? These are philosophic distinctions you
have taken up so often that my inquiry seems to lack distinc-
tion. I don't know where I begin or end. Consciousness eats
up every visual detail in life, but where is it located? These days
I wonder who is living me. When I go out I am walked down
the street, I don't walk. I keep thinking I left Dorian Gray
back there in a club, and that I have never reclaimed him.
Maybe he is somebody else, someone who is living another life.
I may have left him behind on my travels. Or perhaps I am still
confined to your novel. You may never believe I have existed.
Your conception of me is perhaps that of a confused person
who has come to identify with the character in your novel.
Someone obsessed by your theme to the point of voluntarily
living it out. And it is still possible I am that. When I leave
here I will go to Venice. You will understand why. I shall prepare the way of my death.'

Dorian could see Wilde drop his eyes. They were like liquid
jet receding into the marine labyrinth of Venice. Something

had hit a resonating chord in him, it was traced out in a series of inner connections that had him push two knuckles to his lips as a sustaining pivot. He was caught in the instant of being surprised by memory. A cell had imploded into a reflectively disturbed visualisation.

'I pity you more than I do myself,' said Wilde. 'We are both shadow creatures. I have left prison for a scandalous exile. My life is over. I have received my punishment. You have the apprehension that yours has not yet begun. Prison taught me the reverse side of my sentence. The real criminals are the administrators of prisons. Prisoners go through a tunnel, which absolves them, into the light. In the process they become redeemed. I could tell you of this. I wrote a long letter in prison. One day you may read it. In saying this, I mean you will live to read it. One should live as if there were no death, and die as if one had never lived.'

Dorian looked up, and Wilde was no longer with him. He had returned to a subjective tangent and the hum of his inner dialogue. He was somewhere else and wasn't going to come back. Dorian busied himself pouring out another glass of champagne, and then withdrew to a table in the corner. The barman winked at him, his earrings shaking like brilliants. Dorian packed Wilde's conversation and ambience into his head. He wanted to remember everything, and to have all of it on recall. The club was beginning to fill up, and Wilde had been joined by a draggy youth, whose camp manner lit up the bar with raucous histrionics. Dorian could see that neither knew the other, and that the boy was coming on to Wilde as though thrilled by his conquest of the iconic proponent of homosexual love. They were already holding hands, and Dorian could see how Wilde's life had become one of meeting casual acquaintances. His loneliness would have him settle for any casual pick-up or perhaps conquest. Dorian realised that for once his looks had failed him. Wilde had only a passing interest in the figure he had created. Dorian attributed this to the possibility that Wilde knew he would die soon. Facing the probability of his death, he wanted only to be passing through, and to avoid commitments of all kinds.

Dorian continued to watch the two out of the corner of his eye. He had seen the youth somewhere before. Everyone was recognisable in their circle. The boy had a pink rose tattooed on his neck, and his eyes were brushed with a matt black mascara. Wilde was evidently enamoured by the boy's feminine accoutrements. They held hands periodically, and still another bottle of champagne was brought to the table. Wilde was beginning to show signs of being drunk. Dorian could hear his voice climbing an octave, becoming exhibitionistically competitive, aphorisms thrown like dice across the table. 'How evil it is to buy love, and how evil to sell it, and yet it's the best marriage' he could hear Wilde saying. 'The only way to resist temptation is to yield to it,' he was telling the boy with self-deprecatory laughter. The boy lit Wilde's cigarette with attentive, fastidious elegance. He was seducing the older man with all the expertise of a hooker. The boy would periodically rest his head between his elbows on the table and bring his teasing lips close up to Wilde's. Their being together bled with a desperate sense of irreconcilability. The boy was on the make, and Wilde *had* to be acknowledged. The boy was trying on Wilde's gold signet-ring, fitting it to his finger with the expectation that Wilde would say: 'Keep it. It looks better on you.' The boy held out his ring finger to Wilde, and begged the latter's approval. The boy was attempting to persuade Wilde to dance, but he wouldn't, and rooted himself deeper in his chair to resist the advances.

Failing in his effort to have Wilde join him, the boy took to the floor, dramatically lifting his arms, holding the ring up on display and working his body like a torch towards the climactic agony of unrequited love. Wilde looked on with amused disdain, clearly sighting that this wasn't the person for him, but still unwilling to let go the game. The boy danced in a histrionic manner, the tempestuous make-believe of his gestures enforcing the lack of any correlation between himself and the cultured older man drinking to assuage his damaged nerves. The boy used the entire floor space, his movements calculated to impress, every eye in the bar burning into his act, as though he was directing the way towards immediate apocalypse.

Dorian could see that Wilde was losing some of his interest

in the pick-up. The potential for hysterical instrumentation in the boy was manifest in his every gesture. He was clearly someone who would delight in throwing scenes. He would be a volcanic core of mercurial tantrums. Dorian watched him arch his back and project a high-kicking leg. His sexual temerity stopped the bar. The Negro barman froze in the preparation of a blue cocktail. His mouth ovalled into a rictus as he stood back arrested by the boy's provocation, who all the time had eyes for no one but Wilde, who in turn laughed to detract from a situation in which he no longer felt comfortable. Dorian could see it had all gone too far. The boy was another instance of vampishly dressed-up rent.

Dorian was also being approached by a prospective partner. A vamp had come to sit at the table next to him, and was making big eyes through the almond shapes created by eyeliner. An instinctively activated paranoia had him retreat into himself. Nadja had set up a contracting mechanism of self-defence in him, and he had no intention of going back with a possible decoy.

Dorian looked across at Wilde, whose attempts to compensate for a fallen stature in life were palpably makeshift. Prison had blasted inroads into his confidence, and Dorian could assess the infectious vivacity which must have burnt at Wilde's core before he had been so radically dislodged from his psychological pivot. There were flashes of spontaneous exuberance counterbalanced by irreverent maxims, but the big push of his field had gone. Wilde was a precarious survivor in exile, and one whose propensities were becoming increasingly misanthropic. Dorian had a vision of how Wilde must be alone at night, when he returned to his hotel room, an inestimably sad man probably unable to confront his face in the mirror. Someone sitting on the edge of the bed, too despondent to go through the ritual of undressing, hunting through the few envelopes left for him in the hope of finding cheques. He would have returned with a bottle, and would pour himself a cognac before contemplating getting into bed. Dorian imagined him with his head in his hands, telescoping back to his life before prison, and then incredulously fast-forwarding towards an impossibly uncertain future. The hotel room would be frugal – a bed, a table, minimal utility. Perhaps there would be flowers brought by a friend to insert colour into monochrome surroundings. Dorian got this psychological read-out from Wilde's strained nerves, and the way he needed drink to relocate his aphoristic wit.

The boy was still demanding a spotlit attention. He was vulgarising himself in Wilde's eyes with each new attempt to impress by impromptu movements. There was contemptuous applause from some of the tables, and laughter from others, but the boy was locked into his performance and oblivious to external events. His eyes were staring and dilated. He looked manic in the charge he directed towards the large man seated in a chair and attempting to dematerialise. Things were at breaking-point. Dorian expected to see Wilde abruptly leave, and suddenly people were backing off as the dancer pulled a knife from his clothes and directed the point towards the imperturbably staring Wilde. Dorian watched the boy's eyes dance along the blade. He had suddenly added the potential for violence to his auto-eroticised dance, and power was translated into his increasingly dynamised performance. Dorian would have headed for the exit, but he was not going to leave Wilde in this vulnerably exposed state. No one dared approach the boy, the club was frozen into an immobilised silence. Speech and actions were cut dead. The boy continued to make use of the whole floor space, but his eyes never left Wilde, nor did the directing knife-point. Dorian wondered if the boy had been provoked by some minor rejection on Wilde's part, or if he had misconstrued a witticism for personal insult and overreacted by defending a narcissistic pride. Whatever motive had instigated the knife could only be out of all proportion to the events preceding it.

The air tautened as if it were about to snap. The boy narrowed his circle on Wilde's chair, all the time crackling with a dynamism that left him untouchable. He was power voltage about to blow. If someone had touched him, they would have been blackened on the instant. He was caught up in what appeared to be a psychotic game. All of Wilde's inveterate hauteur was needed not to react and so incite violence. The boy was on a madly spinning prowl. He was staring into himself, his only external point of connection being Wilde. There was a weird hum in the air as though his nerves were wired to ignite. Wilde never flinched. The knife and the ring glinted as points of hyperactive light.

The boy got in nearer. His dramatics of dance were being replaced by a channelled objective to focus threat on Wilde. Dorian wondered if the boy was a disturbed homophobe, someone who wore drag in order to gain access to the men who would become the victims of his deranged fixation. He brushed the blade with his lips and executed a dramatic throw-back of his head. He had slowed his rapid circling and was no longer stalking Wilde's table. People brushed up towards the exit as he cleared a chair away with his foot. Events hung on a still unresolved crescendo.

Then it happened in an accelerated flash. Someone came up on the youth suddenly like precipitated lightning, kneeing him in the spine so as to bring him down flat, the knife jumping away and being retrieved, two of the other guests grabbing him by the shoulders and legs before the dilatory club security men arrived to take over.

At that moment Wilde got up, bowed to the people who had come to his assistance, raised his champagne glass and collectedly made for the stairs to exit. Dorian followed. He did not want to be around if the police were called to the club by the security men. He followed Wilde up the stairs, the writer walking with an impaired step, one hand going up to an ear which appeared to have been injured in prison. Unconscious he was being followed, Wilde relapsed into a natural distribution of obstructed energies. The dysfunctional person surfaced, the one he was at pains to bury in company. The man who walked up the stairs was cumbersome, climacteric, seemingly in a state of irretrievable physical degeneracy. He aged ten years with each stair. Dorian could hear Wilde gasping from the exertion. When he got out to the avenue, Dorian placed a hand on his shoulders. A steadying, supportive hand, one that affirmed a sense of being able to go on in adverse and uncompromising conditions. Wilde looked at Dorian in profile and said, 'It's nothing. The boy is not even interestingly mad. The mad are out here in the street.'

Wilde was anxious not to be detained further. Dorian could see he wanted to get away and be by himself in the deepening night. Dorian was determined to risk it. 'I can make a comfortable apartment available to you in my absence,' he said. 'Aspects of it are rather like those you describe in your novel. If you wish, you can come back and look at it now, before making a decision. I don't mean to sound presumptuous.'

Wilde stopped in his tracks. 'I have an unabating need of luxury,' he replied. 'Transform my life and you will transform yourself. I will accept your offer to come back and look at the apartment. After what I have suffered, I need its contrast, unlimited comfort.'

They crossed Paris in a cab. Wilde was taciturn and buried himself deep in his interior. Dorian could see that he was more badly shaken by the incident at the club than he would ever divulge. He was suddenly old and tired in contrast to the youthful figure he had tried hard to project in the club. He looked as though he could let go of life on the instant. The cab encountered a shower. A fast staccato rap of drumheads beat on the roof. A sporadically accelerated hit of percussive crystal flashed off the windows and bodywork as the vehicle bit into the night road. Dorian relaxed into the sensation of speed. Neons, logos kaleidoscoped into jerky cryptograms. The city was nothing but a series of abstract geometries, an architecture of diverse imagery, conflicting ideologies, the whole concentrated amalgam of private and corporate lives grounded or verticalised into scrambled apartments. Blue and red streamers of light chased across the speeding cab. The rain increased and decreased, the cab was hot metal burning through side-streets and coming to an abrupt halt at the lights. A red light stared with conical fixity at the vibrating vehicle. Dorian would have liked to place his hand in Wilde's. He would have liked to offer it as an act of comfort. But he did not dare. The cab took off again, the driver not checking the speed for the obstructively torrential rain. He slammed the cab forward into an aureoled dazzle of sheeting rain.

Dorian no longer cared about safety. There was nothing to lose, any more than there was for Wilde. The two men might have been sealed into a reciprocal death pact. Aimed for a collisional future, they retreated into the precincts of inner space. Dorian was aware of how much out of time he lived, and he could see it was similar for Wilde. Dorian's life constellated around past atrocities. He could not get any real distance on his obsessions. Wilde too was clearly polarised into psychic visualisation. The re-creation of violent trauma ate up energy. Dorian was looking at Basil's incredulously staring eyes in the moment before his consciousness cut out. Then the cab was going forward again, burning the road at speed, the rain thrown off the convex roof as a wooshing sibilant percussion. They were travelling even faster, the driver gunning the pedal as though he was committed to a kamikaze auto-destructive apocalypse.

Wilde was still withdrawn deep into himself. He showed no inclination to speak. He kept his head averted, his consciousness appearing wholly preoccupied by the rain. There was a killing persistence to it. It was like universal applause expressed only through knuckles.

Dorian could recognise nothing through the solid brilliance of the rain. The lights were like paint settling on water. Everything washed into a soluble zigzagging blur. Red, orange, blue and green lights failed to connect with the eye. Dorian felt insulated by the night rain. He let go the notion he was being watched. Nadja's eye had temporarily shut down. Dorian rested in the idea it could not get through. But it was open inside his head. A green almond flecked with red shot. And eyes like that stayed open for ever. They stared out of one century into another. They penetrated walls, fog, skin, every degree of obtrusive opacity. Dorian could feel a buzz in the back of his head alerting him to Nadja's eye. It was a little psychic bleep. It went on and off in a punctuated discourse. A series of impulses which had established their own resonance. Over the past week Dorian had got used to the psychic bleep. He assumed Nadja was typing in subliminal data. Things were being done to his unconscious. He feared the implants would take effect as madness. It would be Nadja's way of cracking him. An insidious means of channelling menace into his back-brain.

The cab came to an abrupt halt again. A red light was splashed on the windows, a rubbed-out radial star suspended in wash.

Wilde looked as though he was ten thousand miles back in his head. He was somewhere else in a state of concentrated distraction.

The cab picked up speed and the rain abated suddenly, held off for a minute and then blindingly returned. A sonic roar opened up around the cab, the detonative light of millions of impacting globules. Dorian could see a tomato being sliced on a white dish, and the sequence changed to an incident from his London days, a Chinaman encountered in a Limehouse opium den, a vignette in which Harry was sitting in the dark waiting for him a year ago, his orange shirt glowing like a fish in an aquarium. Images crystallised before dispersing. They were a part of continuous formation and deformation. Assemblage and disassemblage.

The cab took the length of a sizzling avenue, bucking the sparkling wall of sustained sibilants. They were moving at speed again, the lights fizzing as geometric fractures, the night breaking up around them. It was like looking at scrambled brain cells, Dorian reflected, his whole archetypal substrata blowing into continuous chaos. Wilde was still contained in a psychic microcosm. Whatever he was reviewing was intensely painful, for Dorian watched occasional tears track down his cheeks. He felt the huge isolation that surrounded every individual. The separation of one inner life from another. The experiential pain that divided them at this moment was inestimable. If there had been a glass wall between them it would have extended to the sky. It would have been the width of America. Neither would have seen or heard the other. Dorian kept jolting backwards and forwards from the past to the present. And it was the first time he had experienced this simultaneous process. The rain was being blasted across the cab roof, as though a hose was nozzled into impacted iridescence. Dorian nurtured the night ride with Wilde. It was part of the extended ritual he had contemplated, never quite imagining that it would be realised in this way.

And without warning it was Wilde who placed his hand in Dorian's. He did it quietly and affirmatively, as though confirming their mutual distress, and by joining their hands establishing a bridge of trust between them. This simple bond spoke for their deepest suffering. Wilde again averted his head, and communicated through the informing pressure of his fingers. The driver opened up again and the cab accelerated crazily up the boulevard, Dorian's head rocking from its jolted displacement. The cab was flying. It seemed as though they had jumped out of time and hung suspended in a warp. They were burning across a maze of streets, left, right, a perpendicular chop, a horizontal trajectory. A brake-squealing series of stops and starts.

Dorian felt fired up by a new impulse to live and to escape Nadja's insidious hold. He would get clear of Paris tomorrow. He would travel without once looking back, and then perhaps, he told himself, the bleep in his head would diminish and recede. There would be something and then nothing. He would be free. He tried to imagine freedom as he had known it, as if he had ever known it, as something like sitting on a yellow-poppied beach under a widely escaping sky, no one around, nothing to do, a dinghy tied up on a mooring-rope to a black and white jetty.

Dorian reaffirmed his pressure on Wilde's hand, while the cab seemed to cliff-hang again as the rain whizzed over the roof, the vocabulary in Wilde's hand tapping out nervous instructions, imparting perhaps a fear of the driver as much as a retrospective terror of the past.

When the cab came to an abrupt halt, Dorian assumed they were home, only for the speed to be taken up again, as though the city had expanded to a Chinese box of complicitous puzzles, one intricacy leading to another, the labyrinthine mosaic connected by a series of lights, signals, directives, in the thrust towards the given destination. Dorian assessed that the cab-driver was using the rainstorm to provide a circuitous route to their intended address. Wilde's hand seemed to confirm the lack of trust in direction, and the rain increased its pitch, a resonating volume that sounded like surf pouring across the advancing cab. Orange and blue lights thumbed at the windows like browsing fish. Again, they took off on a foreshortened trajectory, the lack of linearity in their journey adding to the sense of unreality established by the downpour. They could have been riding on the bottom of the sea. The headlights showed in their long orange feelers through the parting traffic. There was a hold-up, and then fluid progress, fast and uninterrupted for what seemed like a long period. The city was being dissected into a series of fragmenting planes. Lights again blazed on the windows. Wilde appeared to be lapsing into drowsiness, he came in and out of consciousness, his eyes focused and then drifting wide of the immediate. The cab-driver uttered an unintelligible exclamation and the cab ground to a halt. Dorian fished for a wad of notes and helped Wilde out his side of the cab.

The rain was still slamming down as they got into the building's entrance hall. Wilde was overtly relieved by the luxury that the furnishings implied, the ormolu and marble interior, the carpeting the colour of red autumn leaves, the Louis XV chair placed as an elegant supernumerary in the anonymously stylised space, the air subtly invaded by a hint of vetiver, and insulating silence separating the building from the street and the world. To Dorian, the return home to the security of that building was akin to being extracted from time and the auditory universe. It meant coming home to himself, a return to sanctuary. He could see Wilde's facial muscles relax, as though his nervous mechanism was reattuning to sympathetic harmonics. He closed his eyes and held out his hands, as if his fingers were orchestrating sensitised light.

Dorian guided him towards the elevator, and he hung back momentarily from encountering himself in the mirror. Dorian watched the black crease ride his features on contact with his image. Wilde was caught out in a brief caption of self-loathing, an encounter with his ageing body. Dorian avoided himself and placed a hand on Wilde's shoulder as they began a slow ascent to the building's fourth floor. Dorian reflected on how many times he had returned at dawn, stepped into the elevator and consulted his drained image in the mirror. He had ritualised his return to privacy in that way. He had sniffed himself out, before consulting hermetic books in his sealed room. He had grown to fear what he saw, and now in Wilde he sensed a similar fear of retrieving self-image. And knowing that Harry would not be there, Dorian was relieved to be returning with someone to his empty apartment. He planned to present Wilde with the keys in the morning and then disappear for ever.

To Dorian's sense-associations, the apartment smelt of Harry's desertion. Something huge had gone, leaving in its place a subtext of split nerve-endings and incomplete dialogue. Wilde must have felt it too, for he lit a cigarette, avoided Harry's blue velvet chair, and said in a resigned voice, 'I see you are alone.'

Dorian poured Wilde the large cognac he requested. A vintage cognac that sat in the glass like woods in October sunlight. Wilde savoured it like the evocation of a past he could no longer trust. They were both exhausted, and Wilde's conversational exuberance had gone dead. Dorian showed Wilde to the sumptuously gold and purple guest-room. The curtained bed loaded with violet silk cushions could have stepped out of his novel. It seemed like a resacralised footnote to his fiction to show him reacquaintance with the luxury that his sensibility desired. Wilde entered the room as naturally as if it had been prepared and waiting for him all his life. He lifted up his arms to what he saw. Dorian opened a sliding wardrobe and took out a mauve satin gown. He held it against Wilde for approval, delighting in how the latter responded with complicitous ease to the notion of drag, his face and body relaxing with a sense of realised identity as he contoured the dress to his body.

Wilde's sense of immediate integration lit up the room. 'I'm too large now for these games,' he responded, hanging on to his note of laughter and expanding it into augmented hilarity.

Dorian took over the dress and stood provocatively confronting himself in a mirror. It was the first time he had looked long and hard at himself for years. He recognised the twisted planes of his beauty, the flawed axis on which he depended for external looks. There was something about him which compulsively magnetised whoever came near, and perhaps it occurred to him it was because of the visible contention in him between self-abuse and perfected good looks. It was the contradiction in him of the whip and the rose, the hidden scars on his body and the inviolable sensitivity in his eyes and high cheekbones that compelled people to stare at his face. He caught all this in an instant, a concertinaed flash of recognition, compulsion and repulsion registering in his eyes with Wilde as the silent onlooker, reading into Dorian still another momentary estimation of a shifting character.

Dorian opened the wardrobe fully and riffled through a rail of expensive dresses, gowns, jackets, a peacock blaze of fabrics which danced along his excited fingertips. It was a fetishistic appeasement of his to be excited by clothes. He had worn all of these outfits, and would now let them go to be replaced by others in the new life he envisaged for himself in Venice. He hoped Wilde would gain a solitary pleasure from extracting garments from his wardrobe and measuring them against himself in front of the mirror.

Dorian left Wilde to rest. He would write him a letter and leave him the keys. He planned to be gone at dawn. He set about preparing his private papers and filled a valise with what he considered to be indispensable documents. He disassembled the altar in his closed room. His private library of erotica would have to remain, at least until he could arrange for its transportation to wherever he set up base. His wealth was independent of his assets, so he felt no apprehension at leaving his apartment.

He wrote Wilde a valedictory letter, explaining that he would be gone possibly for ever, and offering him unlimited use of the apartment. He had received the redemptive light for which he was searching. The curtains in the opposite apartment were wide open, but that was a thing of the past. Already there were hints of dawn in the sky. The stars were showing in their mineral orbits, radials that burnt greenly in deep space. There was a suspension in the air which lives in cities in the hour before daybreak. Even the stream of intermittent cabs had thinned out. Dorian welcomed the reprieve this interval afforded. He stood at the window a last time and looked out at the city coming clear in the blue light. He missed Harry's coming up behind him and placing his hands on his shoulders. He needed to live, and to do that he had to go. Life still appeared possible. An impulse that registered in his brain told him he would survive. It was just light when he slipped out, leaving Wilde asleep.

 *Chapter 4*

HE could not remember a time when the heat was not on him. In every alley he expected to encounter Nadja in a white dress, a knife in his hand and a red carnation behind his ear. The suffocating presence of the canals, their dark-green waters trafficking toxic effluvia and gondolas, served as an associative catalyst to invade Dorian with his past.

Florentino sat crouched on the floor. Dorian extended his right foot, and Florentino began by painting the big toe a polished scarlet and, narrowing his eyes to prevent any inconsistency in the brushwork, proceeded to lacquer the rest of the toenails one by one. Dorian delighted in this cosmetic pedicure. In his own circle in Venice, the court of transvestites over which he presided, Dorian appeared with his fingernails painted red or black, and often in full make-up. He had become the proclaimed apotheosis of transvestism.

Florentino let his black hair pour over his eyes, an obsession that he periodically corrected by throwing back his head and clearing his long fringe. He worked assiduously on Dorian's nails, his long mascara-thickened eyelashes throwing shadows on his cheeks. From time to time he looked up, expecting some note of approval, but received none. Dorian's sadism gave no hint of human contact. He was consumed by his inner preoccupations. Florentino seemed as far away as a star. Dorian had cultivated the art of living in the moment, extending the pulsating nanosecond to a full beat and living with it to the exclusion of an anticipated future. At the back of his mind was not only the fear of Nadja, but the apprehension that he would encounter someone from his past. Somebody at some stage would inform on the bizarre characteristics of his life-style. And there were the nocturnal sex rites over which he officiated on the cemetery island, San Michele, he and his transvestite initiates being rowed out to the island under cover of dark in two black gondolas heaped with violet and red velvet cushions, death ships navigating a passage across the lagoon.

Dorian coldly alerted Florentino to the need to go out and buy household provisions. They needed candles, champagne, flowers, the little things that subscribed to Dorian's extravagant life-style. Florentino looked up in the hope of receiving some note of warmth in Dorian's eyes and voice. They had agreed to push perversity to its limits and marry as two men in a secret ceremony in a private chapel down on the Lido. The marriage would be substantiated in a week's time, but as the date got nearer so Dorian proved increasingly frigid with his emotions, and implacably sadistic in their shared life. Florentino construed this as resentment on Dorian's part to emotive commitment. He had seen men react similarly to women. As the day grew nearer their unconscious hostility found expression in a tempered reserve, an increasing detachment from the union they were about to legitimise. Dorian was manifesting every nuance of his maladjusted emotional spectrum. The twisted jabs that his words imparted, the unpredictable shifts of his radically disordered moods, his deliberate translation of good currency into bad, his annihilative rages, the entire holocaust of his deep-centred complexity found its savage focus in Florentino.

Florentino finished painting the little toe on Dorian's right foot and placed it to dry on a cushion. 'What about the other foot?' he inquired. 'Don't you wish me to do that one? You may not be in the mood to have it done by the time I return. I'd rather do it now,' he risked.

Dorian looked away contemptuously. 'It means nothing to me,' he said. 'Do it or leave it, I couldn't care less. And anyhow, I want my left foot painted black.'

Florentino took up the opportunity to continue, hoping to find an inroad into Dorian's hostile defences. He was searching for a break in the closed circuit that would allow for a return to the mutual sympathy which had brought them together. He selected a bottle of black nail varnish and removed Dorian's gold leather shoe and violet sock. He cradled the extended foot with all the sensitivity of a lover, mapping out meridians and separating the toes preparatory to working on them. Dorian remained expressionless. His eyes were looking up at a high window, the dusty sunlight pouring through the triangular panel above the heavy red curtain. The light was blocked out as a foreign entity, although it afforded Dorian a strangled pleasure occasionally to view an edited stream of sunlight making its way into the apartment.

'Can't you show any affection, Dorian?' Florentino whispered. 'Why are you so hostile? Aren't we to be married soon? Treat me as a lover, not a stranger.'

'Isn't a lover also an enemy,' Dorian acceded in an inflexionless voice. 'You know so little about me. If I were to tell you my real story, you wouldn't be here.'

Florentino tried again to open a rift in Dorian's closed discourse. He tried to imagine something of Dorian's shadow side, and the inexhaustible possibilities contributing to his buried narrative. He inwardly questioned his own refusal to be deeply suspicious about so many of Dorian's behavioural patterns. He had lived blind side up to his lover's sexual aberrations, never questioning that their activating source might be dark. He had refused to question what he lacked reason to find. Dorian represented still, deep waters. The ruins sunk into those depths he had left unexplored. If there was an octopus at the centre feeding on an insoluble diamond, he had left it undisturbed to ingest the conundrum. Images of Dorian as a horned apotheosis presiding over a naked convention of lost children flashed through and out of his mind. Dorian often wouldn't take him out at night, preferring as he put it to consort with the dark alone, and now Florentino's mind was invaded by all manner of lurid suspicions.

'Why are you attracted to someone as perverse as me?'

Dorian asked in a voice of measured detachment.

'Because I love you,' Florentino replied, his mind racing with images of childhood and the aspirations he had nurtured in that uncorrupted state. He thought of his mother's unconditional love and of simple domestic scenes, bread being baked in the kitchen, the winter cold blueing his knuckles, and his mother blowing them warm. He retrieved the loaded fruit-bowl in his mind, and divided the scents of mango, orange, lemon, grapes, peach. His mother would be reading Flaubert or Balzac, or any one of the French novelists, her chair pulled into the sunlight streaming into the room. Only it was not a dusty, inhibited sunlight like the one filtering through now, but an open, generous abundance of light. One in which the scent of fruit circulated. He could smell again the red geraniums massing in the window-box next to blue violas. And there was the moment in which he had exchanged all this for the shadow into which he had drifted. It all came back to him as he concentrated on beautifying Dorian's toenails with a little brush. He could see the jetty in the late afternoon light. There were a number of men grouped beneath it, and he had hung around compelled by a hypnotic fascination to know what brought them to this site. What he had loved was the mask that Venetians adopted as a natural statement of ambiguous gender. And that obsession had persisted. In the evenings he would put on masks indoors or celebrate their imposing symbolism in his nocturnal itinerary of the city's interior. The high moments in his life were when he encountered masked individuals, a blaze of feathers and sequins and abstract facial configurations concealing the identity beneath. Florentino collected masks, and his exotic assemblage constellated his bedroom like the crazy blue-printed mosaic of a species awaiting realisation in the unresolved future. He was still a child at heart, and something of his immediate innocence was translated into his love of masks. They gave him a vantage-point from which to dramatise his love of ritual.

He continued in his slow-motion application of nail lacquer, Dorian observing with pleasure the contrast between the red toenails of one foot and the black of the other. And if Florentino recognised cruelty in Dorian, he had similarly blanked out the possible associations with a disturbed source. He had thought of it as a characteristic which would be modified by love, and which in time would lose its angular edges and be integrated into a smoother construct. He felt his naïvety goose-bump on his skin. It was visible like a nettle-rash. His mind was suddenly invaded by all the possibilities he had previously refused to entertain. It occurred to him that Dorian was tainted. He was made aware that this man carried destruction with him and was vampirical. He needed constant transfusions of youthful blood in order to animate his deleterious organism. Florentino wondered if this was not the attraction of a vampire. Dorian's fangs were internalised in the needle-sharp connections of his neurons.

Florentino stopped his work, and looked up. 'Why don't you stay in tonight?' he asked. 'Do you always have to go out and leave me? Couldn't we be together, just this once? I never know where you go, or who you see. Don't you know I worry? Let's have a fire tonight, and sit by it and dream. We'll scent the logs with orange and cinnamon. It'll be like Christmas.'

Dorian had turned his head away. Florentino could see that he was not going to concede a fraction of his private mythopoetised universe. He was the lion guarding that precinct. His strictures were unencroachable, and he would rise in flames in defence of his territory. Florentino was afraid of Dorian's protracted silence. There was a hint that when it broke, the lion might leap. But Dorian's disdain was expressed through all the mental formulations which remained concealed. He looked at Florentino rather than spoke, directing his voice through his eyes as an instrument of remorseless torment. And when he spoke it was as if he were addressing a stranger.

'We do our own thing at night,' he said. 'I don't interfere with your life, so keep out of mine. We spend our days together and our nights apart. Hasn't that been agreed?'

'I'm growing frightened of what you may do at night,' Florentino responded. 'I dread letting you go out, but I would fear even more following you. I don't think a lover deserves that. I'm growing to hate the nights, and you the days. Can't we spend just one night together. It's impossible like this.'

'So impossible,' said Dorian, 'that you want to marry me.'

Florentino again let the silence pour in. He could feel little darts of fire come alive on the air. Orange signals that pulsed with auric malevolence. He could sense Dorian's impermeable magnitude. There was no rerouting of his emotions; he lacked the disposition to consider any emotive issue in the light of sympathetic adjustment. His eyes and lips denoted inflexible self-worship. And Florentino's disquiet was offset by memories of his first meeting with Dorian, the latter's hair gelled to a quiff, one stylised strand escaping over his forehead, the red silk handkerchief in his breast pocket showing like a sail on the windless lagoon in July. Florentino remembered the whole elated confusion of meeting. His own black hair tumbling in the wind, the red blouse on a girl going by picked out like a cluster of 3D poppies in the water, the whole weight of a partially submerged city distilled around them on the canal, the cupola on St Mark's dipping into low-flying cloud. He was living it all again. The cool tang of wine in his mouth on the café terrace, the air Dorian gave of owning the city, and the way he had periodically removed his dark glasses to emphasise his almond-shaped blue eyes, the most beautiful eyes Florentino had ever seen. Dorian's absolute sense of control, and his way of focusing all his attention on Florentino, had created a magnetic hold from which Florentino could not free himself. They had watched gondolas slip lazily down the ivy-green canals, a wind giving tendrils to the current, the tourists hanging on to the unreality of the funerary city with banged-up eyes. Time had stood stock-still as in a photograph. And Dorian had modulated the balance of his sympathies with perfect control. He had shown just so much invincible reserve in proportion to romantic coercion. Florentino reflected how Dorian had looked even younger with his sunglasses snapped momentarily over his eyes as he glanced towards a brutal patch of glare that had swum through the pack of marine clouds. He tried to equate this Dorian with the one at whose feet he knelt, and the one fitted into the other, although a radical disharmony had occurred in the juxtaposed equilibrium of the two. The man who had initially entered his life, anxious to win his partner, concessionary in almost every allowance, generous in his emotions and sympathetic discourse, had quickly retreated into being an indomitable despot. Having quickly gained a hold on Florentino, Dorian had come to be increasingly reserved, secretive in nature, and sparing in the love he channelled towards Florentino. He appeared always to be punishing Florentino for coming too close. Any act of kindness was succeeded by a perverse one. Florentino felt abused, but his love was irrepressibly directed towards his tormentor. He was attracted towards the snake who, he suspected, would kill him.

He continued to wait for some note of approval from Dorian, his whole life suspended over that void of longing. A kind word would have been enough, but Dorian was typically switched into another dimension. Florentino's nerves were scrambling any attempt to formulate cohesive thought. Everything was disjunctively kinetic and whizzed with explosive impact. Their shared past blew like a meteor. He suffered Dorian's long silences like a count-down evaluating his life. He wanted to reconnect with his past, but its location was situated in mental space, and there was no longer a physical geography in which to find refuge. He was running to nowhere in his head. He was confronting all the crazy configurations of a life lived desperately and to the full, despite its lack of offering any form of security. He wanted to hang on to Dorian's lip, and find in each word an event, a new day charged with expectation.

'My days and my nights are lived by two different people,' Dorian said out of nowhere. 'I can only give you one and not the other. We are all divided, even in love. . . .'

He was interrupted in speaking by their houseboy, Fabio, coming into the room to announce the arrival of callers. Dorian looked confused and on instant alert. His mind was wired to every conceivable portent. And having two young guys shown into the room at the time of a ritual pedicure, made him decide he would fire Fabio that afternoon. At first he did not recognise them, for they were not wearing make-up, and then when he heard Mario's voice he realised they were part of his intimate retinue. They were two of his night associates demythicised by their daytime appearance. Mario was wearing a black beret, and the only clue to his nocturnal identity was the little gold earring that danced in his right ear. He was with Paul, an English boy, who had come to live in Venice for the tolerance granted his sexual propensities. They both looked so ordinary in their matelot vests and denims that Dorian recoiled from the natural appearance they presented. He was unable ever to let go his artificial image, and refused to compromise for any social convention. He did not want Florentino involved in this matter, and quickly showed his two callers into another room. Any overlap from his night-world into the day was a cause for deep consternation. He could feel his natural emotive detachment increase, and his sadism come alive like a wire in his forehead. He paid for deviance in others but did not extend that fiscal arrangement outside of a particular time and place. He was not even sure how they had secured his address, and it was only disquiet over their having got hold of him that made him temper the unnerving rage which had intensified to white heat in him. He coldly dismissed Florentino from the room and slammed the door.

'I know we're intruding,' said Paul, 'but we asked around for your address, and managed to get here. There's something going on at the island when we're not there. Someone's on our trail.'

'We went out there yesterday,' intruded Mario. 'I know you told us to keep away from the place during the day, but some impulse took us back. Well, you know inside the ruined chapel, where we use the altar. Someone had been there. Right above the altar there were the words DORIAN GRAY IS THE DEVIL. HE WILL MURDER YOU ALL. And even worse, there was a photograph of you placed in front of two black candles. We cleared the place up . . .'

'But there was someone there,' resumed Paul. 'He was in the thicket of trees as we came out. We could hear him laughing and the sound of branches breaking. We got scared and ran for the boat.'

Dorian listened with no vestige of personal involvement. He was thinking back to the time of his engagement to the actress Sibyl Vane, of her suicide, and Harry's advising him to forget all about her death and disown any feelings of responsibility for it. His heart had set into an impenetrable red ice. He had found then at Harry's instigation a rapacious predilection within himself for detachment. He had disconnected, and never returned to the arena of human feelings. What he experienced now was only a concern for his safety. The people he had used up did not matter. They were a metaphor for his unrelieved sense of boredom.

'It's just some psychopath,' Dorian heard himself saying. 'You get them in every city. Don't be afraid. But I won't have you out there in the daytime. Why have you disobeyed my instructions? I am *not* to be disobeyed.'

Dorian watched his two devotees swallow their shame. They were visibly more frightened of him than what they had encountered out on the island. A tremor lined the upper corner of Mario's lip. Dorian could see that was his breaking-point. It had been like that with Sibyl Vane. And Paul was disquieted by what he had experienced. Little darts of paranoia had been injected into their systems. They had been needled into real fear.

'I don't want to go back there,' said Paul with declarative conviction in his voice. 'We're being watched.'

Dorian stood there measuring the possibilities of Nadja's intruding on their circle. He kept dismissing the idea, attributing the menace to a local weirdo, but finding his notion pulled up by the idea of someone using his name and photograph. Without a doubt he had been traced. News of his life had leaked into the information carried by the inky canals. His past was floating on the waters like a data-based hologram. He imagined seeing his image cloned right across the lagoon: *Dorian Gray.*

To buy time for reflection he ran his fingertips over his silk shirt. The tactile sensuality imparted by that contact brought him some momentary reprieve from fear. He was sighting Nadja in his mind through psychic visualisation. His platinum hair and red lipstick gash were brutally up-front and alarmingly confrontational.

'What else did you discover out there?' Dorian asked through half-closed lips.

'There was some paper money in a bowl which was charred and half burnt as a kind of offering,' Mario rushed out.

'Do either of you know my name?' Dorian asked. 'Do you seriously think the words apply to me?'

'There was this photograph,' said Paul, handing it to Dorian, who scrutinised his own indomitable features, recognising instantly that it had been taken in Paris. The shot had been snapped on a café terrace in the Champs-Élysées, and Dorian in a relaxed mood was unconsciously looking direct into the lens, his dark glasses held elegantly in his left hand, while his right was seen extending for a wineglass. He had been captured in a moment that would never be recorded again – one of the millions that flashed by like photons; the incriminatory nanoseconds.

He examined the photograph with a note of defiant objectivity, and even now in the heat of crisis he was concerned more with his appearance, the way his hair fell, and the unnerving magnetism of his features. He was at once fascinated by this face and the imagined effect it had on others.

'Nothing is going to change,' Dorian said to Mario and Paul. 'We are not going to be frightened away by a voyeuristic pervert. These sort of scares happen all the time.' As he spoke, he could see their vacillation, for it was the powerful stimulant of illicitly ritualistic sex that drove them out to the island at night. Dorian knew that compulsion would have taken them to dark places anywhere, but it was the whole ritual of crossing the waters to a chapel, dressing up, and having sex conducted by him as the master which kept these youths in unflinching subjugation. Dorian remembered how in London men had got up and left the room on his entry into a restaurant or club, because of the infamous gossip circulating about him. His undertow was fished for legitimate scandal. Here he had lived out those speculations, he had personified the role of moral antagonist. Arrest could come at any time, but to date it hadn't. He thought of Aleister Crowley's dictum, 'spiritual attainments are incompatible with bourgeois morality', and savoured the tang of his desperately transient freedom.

'We'll go there for a last time, tomorrow night,' Dorian said in a neutral voice. 'After that, I will choose another equally special place in which to meet. Look around the city and let me know what you think.'

What he could hear was the lack of conviction in his voice. His timbre was flat, and in his mind he was searching to be bigger than the fear Nadja imposed on his freedom. He was anxious to be left alone, and communicated the impulse to Mario and Paul, who, glad to get out of the place, hurried off with the promise that they would be waiting underneath the jetty the following night.

Dorian was left alone under a brutally interrogative mental spotlight. Trapped in its blue laser, he appeared to be encountering the topography of his individual death. There were lions breathing flame running at random through truncated statuary. He was facing out across an apocalyptic landscape. He could not adjust to the reverse electromagnetic field. There was no gravity, so he had the feeling he was inexpertly floating above the ground. His vision was still tunnelled into familiar obsessions. Then he was being dragged back. He was standing outside gates studded with blazing jewels. Emeralds, rubies, sapphires flared with their mineral fires. The gate was guarded by a black snake. The snake had gold, chequered markings on its leather skin. Its head rose and fell in a series of spiral movements. It wanted him out, and Dorian broke sequence and went immediately into the next room where Florentino was sitting, feet up on a couch, reading a book. He found it impossible to compose his inner sense of rage at someone interfering with his life. He construed any form of opposition as personal affrontery. He stood with his hands on his hips in the middle of the room encountering his invisible adversary. He could have paid to have Nadja liquidated, but there would be others and still others who would track him to the ends of the earth.

He sat down and screened his emotions from Florentino. He believed that to show any least concession to cracking would leave him inalienably isolated. Harry had gone, and he had found himself living with Florentino, whom he did not love. That he needed him around was in part because of his fear of dying alone. He had an apprehension of the end, and it was crowded with fear, a cadenza burning through his nerves, his past blazing out to a receding blip of light pulsing above the lagoon. And he wanted a witness, someone there who would know he had lived, no matter how improbably. He had selected Florentino for that purpose. The boy was passively and undeviatingly loyal.

He lived for a bond that involved emotional subjugation. His adjuration to service was a compulsory need. Dorian's desire to marry him was based on a perverse sense of ritual which would undermine the orthodox notion of union. It was something he could not let escape to his partner.

'Florentino,' said Dorian, 'I have decided to put forward the date of our marriage.'

The boy looked up and his eyes were raindropped with tears. His emotions crumpled at this unpredicted surprise. The ingenuous play of his emotions flooded with an unmediated spontaneity. 'Do you really mean it?' he asked, hardly daring to believe in Dorian's unprecedented display of emotional generosity.

'Of course I do,' Dorian replied, attempting to generate emoted charge to his words. 'I have kept you waiting, and the time is right. I will see that the chapel is prepared for next week. And of course we need to decide on your costume. Will it be black or white or flaming red? At any rate, there are a lot of preparations to be made.'

Florentino stood up and leapt into the air. His uncontained joy registered in that exhilarated leap, his two hands clapping together in a stinging flash. Dorian watched the young man choreograph the rush of adrenalin to his system. Florentino was transformed on that instant into a star. And having received the news he so wanted, he rushed out of the room assiduously to set about fetching the necessary household provisions from the neighbourhood shops. His life appeared to be the chemical printout of an uninterrupted future. His informational DNA, his gene pool, his endorphin buzz, his biochemistry were all programmed for a future in which Dorian would share.

Dorian listened to the door bang shut and let the silence build up around him like a lake returning to optimum level after long rain. He felt the silence insulate his being. It was a process always of returning to himself, as though dialogue at the interior was dependent on self-attuned access to inner hearing. It was then that his real world came up. A forest opened to disclose a castle concealed by a deep canopy of green foliage. His psyche was trapped in that castle. He could hear it beating against the walls like a bat in a series of frantic ricochets. A different aspect appeared at every window. All of his complex, multiple inner states showed as a sequence of pathological events. His whole psychological hermeneutics were visible in the configuration of archetypal components. At such times his sense of depersonalisation was acute, he felt separated from any of the informing agents that invested life with a sense of immanence. He felt disconnected, he suffered at such times the absence of a person. He reviewed his psychic index without animation or feeling. His desensitised castle was the repository of dead images hung up like desiccated flies in a spider's ripped web. At times he wanted to scream because he could not connect, and he would have liked a guide or intermediary to point the way into the castle. He needed an angel to fly above the trees, a gold alphabet streaming as a vapour trail behind a fluently instructive trajectory. But the castle was impenetrable. Its turrets, crenellations and spashes of ivy presented a redoubtable face. He was locked out and would have to stay amongst the wet trees at nightfall. He could taste the sense of self-alienation in his mouth. He wondered who and what was living him with such twisted autonomy. He had been let off again and again in his run of good luck. He saw himself as he had been in London, the night Sibyl Vane's brother had confronted him outside an opium den in the East End. He could see red lights showing through the fog. He had been found out, brought face to face with the cutting edge of death, but he had lied his way out, claiming that his youthful appearance would have made it impossible for him to be the Dorian who had been responsible all those years ago for Sibyl Vane's suicide. And his lies still held good. He has been left untouched for the most serious crimes, but he realised that Nadja would never let up. In him he had encountered his true adversary. The road was broken with holes, and at the end of it was a dead drop into white water.

Dorian pulled himself back from the edge and poured a drink. His hands were becoming increasingly unsteady from liquor. He had to assert control over his movements and had become over-aware of his nervous degeneration. He wondered if Florentino would see his inadequacies, or if the boy was too naïve, too close up to be aware of the other's dysfunctional habits. While he could detect no outward change in his features, Dorian could read the pathologised chaos in his nerves. A schizoid pattern was establishing itself in his life. Paranoid delusions induced by the contents of his unconscious and alcohol excess were making serious inroads into his ability to function. And the more he was undercut from the inside, the colder he grew in his external manner. He thought it impossible that anyone could love him. He presented a sense of detachment that would be construed as mystique, and a physical beauty that could be seen as the product of a twistedly inverted aestheticism. Florentino had questioned neither of these conditions. In the past Dorian would have delighted in such unquestionable loyalty, he had got his kicks from a sense of blind worship on the part of his devotees. And the greater the degree of susceptibility on their part, the more he had derived pleasure from walking over the ordinary. At the time he had considered himself to be without need of revision. He had seen his life as a completed index, an open-ended horizon over which he held indomitable charge. But with self-evaluation had come the suspicion that anyone attracted to him was necessarily corrupt or voluntarily entertaining ruin. He questioned Florentino's fascination with so deleterious a source. If he could not perceive the dangers in the liaison, his future was questionable. But Dorian was determined not to let on. He was sufficiently advanced in his pattern of self-destruction not to take others into account. His way was unredeemable, and he would follow it through, right to the steps at the bottom of the darkest alley.

Dorian could hear Florentino returning. His boots resounded in the courtyard, and Dorian could hear him, arms crammed with boxes, excitedly rushing from room to room of the apartment. When he tumbled back into Dorian's presence, he was half elated and half apologetic for his state of manic exhilaration. There was no reciprocally sustainable focus for his joy, and so it was impossible to maintain without hysteric impulse. Florentino dragged the last of the boxes on the floor, the one containing candles, chocolates, and what Dorian could make out as a red velvet beret. What should have been a cause for celebration and the immediate popping of a cork was again neutralised by Dorian's reserve. His immeasurably cool demeanour stood off from any involvement with pleasure.

Florentino did not persist. He had gained the impossible, and was unwilling to risk its loss by further questioning. Dorian watched as the boy's face reverted to its customary seriousness. Florentino was self-consciously recomposing his inner reserve. He needed to readopt the face that was expected of him, the one he used as the predominant mode of expression with Dorian.

'I got a red beret,' Florentino said elatedly. 'It will be part of my marriage costume. Can we choose the clothes later? There are things in your wardrobe I'd like to wear, and I've seen other bits and pieces in town.'

Dorian coaxed the red velvet with his fingertips. He afforded the fabric a lover's caress, while deliberately avoiding contact with Florentino's body. It was his old habit. A propensity for things rather than people. A red beret rather than Florentino's lips.

'We'll choose today,' Dorian asserted. 'Really, the sooner the better. We'll choose something ceremonially exotic. You'll look like the boy-king of the underworld. The one who is dressed for a royal marriage under the midnight sun.'

Florentino looked puzzled at Dorian's words. Something of the boy's suspicions were apparent in his lack of comprehension. What he did not understand he let slip into quizzical drift. Dorian felt uncomfortable that the boy should feel the least hint of suspicion, and to restore his sense of high spirits, put on the red velvet beret at a slouched angle and offered himself to the mirror. The beret crowning Dorian's hair looked a storm. He immediately won the excited approval of Florentino, who then tried it on himself, lowering the beret at a provocative tilt over his left eyebrow, and in turn seeking Dorian's approval.

Dorian took the initiative and had Florentino follow him into the dressing-room with its concealed wardrobes built into panelled walls. A scent was released when Dorian unlocked and slid open the first of the satinwood slide-doors. He had forgotten the opulence of his collection, the textural density of velvets, satins, heavy sequins, clothes he had not worn since his Paris days, and probably would not wear again. Florentino's eyes went huge at the prospect of such rich fabrics. Dorian had

never made his wardrobe available to anyone but Harry, and
now Florentino tugged at a purple velvet jacket, so rich in its
unmarked fabric that even to touch its skin was to appear to
bruise the material. Florentino picked at scarlet, black, blue and
gold alternatives, his taste for extravagance stimulated by the
wealth and diversity of choice. He would have liked to try on
everything, his fascination with Dorian's wardrobe being like a
raid on his lover's mind. So much time and care must have
gone into the assembly of these detailed and fetishistic garments that Florentino saw them as comprising a distinct section
of Dorian's mind.

Dorian fished out a black boating cloak to be worn over the
purple velvet jacket, an ensemble that would be matched with
the red beret and selected jewels. He told Florentino that for
their wedding ceremony he should have a mauve cross dyed
into his hair, as a symbol of their profound union. A transvestite hierarchy would preside over an occultly ritualised ceremony.
The gondolas were to be loaded with flowers. Dorian gave
Florentino only the information likely to appeal to his love of
theatrical ceremony. He would prepare his own clothes on the
day, and adapt them to his concept of funeral rites attendant
on a marital display. In the back of his mind was the prospect
that these were his last days and that he would live them out in
a way that would leave an indelible mark on the microfiche
indexing the inevitable dead. He knew that his life would be
talked about, and that he had thumb-printed human consciousness as it was taken up in the lives of the great story. He would
strike an image that would prove unforgettable to the moment,
and so be recorded in infinity.

Florentino heaped the chosen clothes over his left arm and
walked in an automated fashion back into the next room. It
was his special day, and it provoked a childlike innocence in his
spontaneous nature. Florentino could not speak for apprehension. He looked as though he were counting the lights over
town. Dorian followed uneasily at a distance, his mind con-
figurating schemes that would have cut right across Florentino's
expectations. He was obsessively sighting apocalypse. He saw
himself at the centre of a burning cone from which the big

event telescoped. The parallel dimensions would open out. His consciousness would expand to a cosmic omelette, blackened around the edges. His seething ingredients would impregnate death. In his delusional fantasies he imagined himself led to the highest throne. Angels would back off from his image. He would be everything and nothing.

Florentino was busy trying on clothes, challenging them to fit, adjusting a shoulder, searching for feedback as he looked approvingly at the length of a sleeve, the particular contour of velvet to his waist. Dorian left him to amuse himself. He was thinking of the ravaged portrait, the object that had been the source of all his subsequent troubles ever since Basil Hallward's vision had first given it expression. Basil, Dorian reflected, had set in motion a universal pathology. For a long time he had given no thought to the portrait, but now he was burning with curiosity to know if the painting had repaired itself or further deteriorated. The unmitigated self-hatred he had expressed in attempting to mutilate the painting had left a scar on his extended youth. He had remained almost imperceptibly unchanged, but the beginnings of hair-fine lines around his mouth and eyes were visible to his microscopic scrutiny. He had felt the outward give inside. He knew at any time the whole exterior could crack. He had abandoned caring how old or young he was. He wondered if the portrait would tell him, or if that too would defy him in having any certain hold on reality.

The portrait was concealed in one of his wardrobes. He kept it in a locked safe, wrapped in protective sheets of brown paper. He had the feeling its pigmental decomposition was paralleled in his cellular decay, a process apparently arrested by his looks. He was also afraid of the imparted power alive in the portrait. What if it exploded or autocombusted on opening? He feared psychic recrimination on Basil Hallward's part. Anything could escape from the portfolio. Viral bacteria, a squall of irate and toxin-carrying bees, an avenging acid fired out of the existing left eye into his right, a pollutant ink, or the crackle of static indicating Basil's presence.

Dorian knew the moment was not right. He would re-evaluate his mutilated image after the marriage. Once he had committed himself to the final night, he would re-encounter his shadow, and either draw strength from it or be annihilated by its malevolent reproach. He thought again of the castle from which he was locked out. In a recent dream its towers had been on fire. Someone had been seen waving a burning flag from the ramparts. There were monsters in the dream. A dragon had spat chunky rubies out of its throat. They had hissed into the moat with resounding discharge. Everything had been teleologically chaotic. What he knew in his dissociated state was that he appeared to be no nearer achieving integration. There had been an empty boat on the still green waters of the castle moat. The boat flew a white flag. There was a naked woman sitting in the stern. Her long red hair was tied up with a snake.

He feared the portrait would confirm his negative intuition. He was used up as a psychophysical entity, but dangerously alive in his soul-findings.

He listened to Florentino singing as he tried on his ritual costume. Dorian lit his head up with a crippling tumbler of whisky. His brain fried under the chemical lift-off. He would consult the portrait the day after his marriage. Florentino was still singing. There were fireworks going off over the lagoon. They fizzed on release, tailing off on pyrotechnical arcs. It seemed a fitting prelude to his marriage. He poured himself another whisky, contained his shaking hands and prepared for the events ahead.

Chapter 5

DORIAN did not understand how Harry had succeeded in locating him. The letter, with its familiar handwriting, had found his address. The envelope was postmarked London, and it occurred to Dorian with a jabbing sense of apprehension that Harry must have had a spy out on him, for there was no mention in his letter of how he had come by Dorian's Venice address. Harry had written to say that after a period in Berlin he had returned to London and was now reunited with his wife. He made no mention of the rapid transition he had made in sexual orientation, and mentioned nothing of their past relationship, evidently for fear of incrimination. The letter attempted to make good his present by neutral emotions. His tone was like that of a singer deliberately using unemotive phrasing. But already in the complexity of his thinking Dorian was associating Harry with Nadja. He was certain that it was Nadja's doing that he had been found out. And he imagined Harry in complicity with his transvestite adversary. Even if their encounters had not been sexual, it was Dorian's belief that Nadja must have continued his contact with Harry. During his period of exile Dorian had severed all contact with the past. In every possible way he had seen that his new life was legitimised by exclusive anonymity. He had broken off contact with the scene, and confined himself to an exclusive circle, a court over which he officiated with select members subscribing to rigid vows of silence.

Dorian read and reread the letter, searching for a clue, a buried intimation of some continuing bond between himself and Harry. He felt certain a subtextual meaning was intended, for his continuing capacity to feel hurt at the expense of his former lover was brutally apparent in the rage contracted in his being. But, try as he did, Dorian could discern no sympathetic undertones in Harry's factually minimal account of his life. He had concluded the letter by assuring Dorian that they would never meet again in any circumstances, and he had supplied no address by which he could be contacted.

Dorian felt the bruise turn mauve under his skin. It was the irremediably damaged psychokinetics of his soul which he felt to be beyond attention. He tried to estimate who and what Harry was inside him, and how a relegated love could still permeate his nerves with such stinging hurt. How was it that a relocated, incorporeal force could inject unmitigated pain into his heart. The afterglow of their love carried with it the lethal blaze of a heat-flash. It scorched him to contemplate loss. He had assumed he had adjusted, but once again his emotions had let him down. He crumpled the letter to an impacted ball. Years of his past were contained in that fist-sized paper receptacle. It was like a loaded missile when he threw it hard at the opposing wall. It was also like a blow in Harry's face. He was compounding his rage into that one dynamited gesture. And almost immediately, as a corrective to hatred, came his fear of the possible source of this letter. He imagined Harry and Nadja conspiring together in the time before Harry had fled from Paris. He saw the two of them together in a smoky bar, intimate, burnt by a mutual desire to destroy him. Nadja would have placed lipstick kisses on Harry's ears. He would have scented money and power. To Dorian it had been clear for a long time that the future would always be obstructed by an opponent. The opposition was like a shadow on the road. The sense of apprehension began in the psyche, and later on realised itself as a person. Dorian had known this excerpted subtext to consciousness in all its subtle variants. And when it had composed itself into materialisation in the form of Nadja, it was with ambivalent feelings of relief and terror that he had contemplated his omnipotent double. He had heard music coming out of drains at noon, he had watched the sun simultaneously turn black, he had fainted at the end of corridors under the streets connecting with entrances which appeared to take him out of time.

Dorian brought himself back to the prospects of his imminent marriage. Mario and Paul were to be part of the ceremony, as were the other three members of his retinue, Umberto, Cesare and Jean-Yves, another French boy who had taken refuge in Venice, a city that to Dorian personified decadence. Dorian had supplied each of them with clothes for their nocturnal excesses, costumes that would signify the occult pact he intended to make with demonic energies. He needed to avoid heavy drinking during the day, and purposely locked away the selected range of whiskies inviting his attention. He took out the book he prized above all others, his specially bound copy of Huysmans's *À Rebours*, and flipped at random through some of the passages which had over the years afforded him such pleasure. It reminded him of semen and perfume, incense and ripe hayfields before thunder. He could never tire of the passage in which the protagonist picks up a schoolboy and proceeds to have an unlikely relationship with his chance encounter. Or the passage in which sexual stimulus is incited by the provocation of having a third party bang on the door during the sexual act, issuing threats of being the law come to apprehend the participants. And there was the protagonist's bibliophilic mania, his love of perfumes and precious stones, his strung-out, jaded nerves looking at any condition to alleviate tension. The book had contributed to Oscar's aspects of decadence – and it was the dynamic behind all those who lived on an attenuated sensory plane. Dorian found consolation in riffling through passages he had marked up as particular to his needs. What he fed on was kicks. The sensation of wild speed in his nerves. What he would have liked was a literature that blew the back out of the sky. He had made a ritual burning of all realist novels. It had delighted him in the past to buy up whole stocks of mediocre novels and burn them to grizzled cinders. He had bought his own warehouse and yard for this purpose in London, and helped by two leather kids he had doused wedges of books in petroleum and torched them. He had seen it as a retributive nemesis for dead fiction. By the time he had left the yard it had thrilled him to realise that he had incinerated fifty thousand books in a black lick of smoke curling above the East End. He was additionally inspired in what he saw as an act of universal vengeance, by the prospect of those writers working at night on the new books that would follow the others into the fire. He would singularly eliminate their work. His life had been a series of exalted acts of revenge. His hostility to every form of inherited convention had driven him into the underworld. Tonight he would consummate his extreme hatred of moral dictates by manifesting deviant power.

He had ordered his rooms to be shot through with pink and white carnations and red roses. This floral extravagance was a gift to Florentino, who was deliberately restraining the emotions he felt at the coming ceremony. His usual sassy naïvety was under check. Dorian had evaluated only too well the compensatory opposite taken up by those who feared their own state of happiness. The others he could rely on. Their sexual needs could be supplied only by danger and were heightened by cross-dressing. He thought of how lust drove people into unlikely places, and how it established a global network of complex geometries, people going with and against the grain in all the dark recesses of the day and night. He had looked to find a future king under the bridges.

They would be rowed out to the island at midnight. It was Dorian's intention to stay out there until dawn. Only then would he return, assured of his union with the dark. For a long time Dorian had studied the effects of sexual energies as a means of animating the fire-snake, and of the power generated by a sphincter-movement practised with magical effect and which transmitted current to the subtle workings of the spinal column. And wishing to occultise the practice of anal sex, he had studied this method as an inverted power-zone, in which constant contractions of the sphincter act as an attack upon the fire-snake, which then strikes with its tail at the *conus medullaris.* He had subverted a tantric practice into a debased ritual. Dorian's interests were in trafficking with entities from the abyss. It was the resources of cosmic chaos on which he drew, a whole metadimensional awareness of encounters with insighted agents or extraterrestrials who appeared in sensitised areas of erogenous consciousness.

Dorian pictured the ruined chapel hung with red and black drapes. He was aware of static twitches of thunder which rolled over in the low cloud like surf heard breaking somewhere on a reef. There was a live, seething fizz in the air. He knew the oppressiveness would lift later. What it sounded like was a piano being shifted on bare boards in the sky. What he had lost was a sense of heightened sensation. He could not recharge himself in order to know again the buzzing anticipation of the night to come. He thought of lining cocaine or taking a mixture of drugs, any chemical formula that would heighten consciousness. He decided to delay that until the night.

There was thunder again, only this time the volume was turned up. The decibel wall was walking across the sky. Sonic reverberations crashed in from the ocean. There was storm in the air, which kept coming and going in a syncopated rhythm. But the sound was never fully delivered. To Dorian's mind it seemed that the storm was holding off and that the elemental climax would register when the ceremony was consummated. He had always believed in the power of parthenogenesis or unaided conception, and now in his fantasies over Florentino he imagined their union resulting in the birth of a brainchild. It would in time step out of Florentino's left eye, a child no larger than a gold insect, standing in a tear-duct or balanced on an eyelash, waving its filigree arms and legs like antennae. Florentino would watch it grow from incubation to incubus. It would shiver with iridescent pigmentation, its tiny gold eyes focused on its own conscious perception of the world. And it would grow each year to prove too indomitably intractable to Florentino. Neither orders nor chains would bring the child into obedience.

Dorian engaged himself in this idea of regenerative tyranny, occasionally alerted to reality by the intermittent rumour of thunder and by the sound of Florentino's high register as he busied himself with preparations for the night. The boy's natural falsetto invaded the house. Dorian was growing progressively more disquieted. His nerves bit along his spine and burnt in his stomach. His conflict was with time. How to get the remorseless agony of the existential crisis from one moment to the next. He did not believe his nerves would hold out that long. It would soon be dark. The autumn day was closing to a clammy end. The thunder had gone off like a big cat sated by the kill. There was an absolute stillness in the air, as though Dorian was living under a glass dome. He could hear the metronomic tick of rain that came and went, came and went. The calm embodied tension. Someone was playing a slow, melancholy guitar on the opposite balcony. They could have been composing a chord sequence to his past. The elegiac musical summation to a life hung up like a damaged window in the sky.

Dorian was accustoming himself to the possibility that perhaps all he would ever know of life would be thumbprinted into the next hours. It was his time pitched against the continuity. In the face of possible annihilation he returned to thinking of the power-zones in the subtle body. And the idea of Oscar formed another matrix to his obsessive thought patterns. He wondered if Wilde had continued to use his Paris apartment for temporary refuge, or if after the novelty had worn thin he had returned to living in the cheap hotels in which he prized his anonymity. Oscar, he assured himself, would celebrate the moment in any environment. He would kill boredom by imposing the bizarre on the ordinary. Oscar, who claimed that his one concession to exercise in Paris had been playing a game of dominoes outside a café, had grown to be the degenerate embodiment of lack of physical exercise. Dorian had seen in Wilde's ear injury and partial impairment of balance and speech a premonition of the end. He had imagined their death as being contemporaneous. He saw it as written in the big black book hidden under leaves in the heart of a forest.

Dorian's interests were in the psychosexual substance of the shadow. Opening the *ajna chakra* or third eye as the site of mystical vision of extraterrestrial planes of existence was one way of knowing a different state of reality. The world of appearances disappeared at the opening of this eye, to be replaced by an autonomous stream of phenomenal illusion. Dorian had studied the location of the major *chakras*: the one at the base of the brain, which is the cerebral seat of sexual energy, and the ones in the palms of the hands, which are the sites of intense magical power. He had learnt to tap into the circuit and to liberate transmitted energies, and had in time achieved a mastery of *kundalini*, inciting the fire-snake to branch out along his spine to the various power-zones in the body's subtle text. But it was the secret eye on which Dorian was determined to concentrate, that occult manifestation which was central to the magician's formulaic power. He was fascinated by its association with the goat's anus, and its feminine connotations with the astro-glyph of the scarlet woman. For the male, the magic eye was a symbol of the black arts, an incontrovertibly destructive principle connected to the drive for omnipotence. He had come to learn of the cabalistic cross of the four quarters, the emblem of Baron Samedhi, of Maître Carrefour, the Lord of the Crossroads and the God of the Dead, who is to be evoked before crossing the threshold. Dorian had studied the body as a compendium of magic symbols, and the unconscious as representing the endless permutations of the shadow. He was secure in a knowledge with which he could manipulate his sexual court, and in an auric power that both fascinated and intimidated Florentino.

Now that the dark had dropped down, Dorian felt less shot through with anxiety. Occasionally a warm, saturating rain hissed like a cat over the lagoon. The rehearsed theatrics of his wedding night found a responsive instrumentation in his nerves. He had earlier on checked the two black gondolas in their locked shed by the wharf. They had been prepared to plan, their goldleaf finishings, cushions emblematised with the ibis and the snake, and prows heaped with flowers were ready to be carried out and launched on the night waters. They could cross over to San Michele in absolute secrecy, Dorian forbidding any navigation lights until they were well clear of the city. They would form a transvestite cortège with muffled oars making their inroad into the dark.

And Oscar? He kept on appearing in Dorian's mind. It seemed as if he were reading the impulses that flashed through Dorian's nerves. In Dorian's mind Oscar was walking broodingly through Père Lachaise, contemplating the inscriptions on gravestones. The paths were splashed with autumnal leaves, and his visible consternation showed in the way he had neglected his appearance, as though he was partly reconciled to his coming death. To Dorian's acute sense of psychic perception, Oscar's need to communicate was urgent. Telepathic thumbprints were being keyed into Dorian's neurons. Both men had picked up on communicating crises. Dorian could not free himself of the image of Wilde closing his eyes on some incommunicable pain.

Dorian looked to magic to transcend all existing ties. He had seen the new aeon as characterised by the magical use of semen and mental states represented by erogenous power-zones, rather than connected to the old blood rites of Osiris. Magic promised deathlessness to the triumphant adept. Dorian considered that if he should live, he would devote himself strictly to the study of ritual magic, and acquire the investiture of suprahuman powers it promised. The luminous intrinsic ejaculation achieved through activating the fire-snake was mirrored outwardly in the sex magic Dorian practised with his devotees. He had been warned of the catastrophic consequences of abusing magic power and of using it for inflating the ego. An unbalanced degree of inner illumination would, as Dorian had already and voluntarily experienced, subvert the subtle body and lead to delusional mania. He had chosen to exist on this plane for a long time in acting out sex magic. The proper vibration of sexual energies would, Dorian believed, lead to the conquest of death. And it was in his abilities as a magician that Dorian had conceived of the notion of creating a parthenogenetic child. The potent force of his unconscious imagery impressed on his discharge would instruct the fertilisation to occur in Florentino. He was aware too that only initiated consciousness could survive major and outer catastrophes. By applying to Florentino the ritualised instructions most commonly performed between the phallic power of the magician and his female counterpart, Dorian intended to release accumulated energy to achieve transhuman creation. And with the night building, it would be his night, the one in which a new race would be born through his mental projection. Florentino would go back to Venice carrying the seed of the chosen one.

Dorian reflected on the possibilities of achieving cosmic power. Improbable accidents occurring in the process of conducting a magic experiment were the felicitous pivot on which success depended. The magnetisation of the fire-snake and the use of Florentino were the channels that would lead to ultimate truth. And looking to realise within himself the identities of Shaitan and the black god Osiris, the sexual ordeal or the channelling of psycho-magical energies would take place in secret between himself and Florentino. It was during the final sublimation that they would be screened from the other neophytes at the altar. Florentino would also represent the jackal-headed god, Anubis, for the form of sex appropriate to that symbol. This time Dorian knew it would all come right. The great work would be effected, even if it resulted in his death.

Dorian attributed his own immutable looks and largely invincible health more to the practice of magic than to the freak associations surrounding his portrait. It was a side of his life that he had kept separate from Harry, both in London and in their shared life in Paris, and one which he had kept well hidden from all the casual pick-ups who had come into his life. Magic had grown increasingly to be the true focus of his identity. It was a solitary pursuit, and the degree of psychological monitoring required on the part of the adept was ideally suited to Dorian's increasingly introspective sensibility. Now more than ever Dorian required total power. On overreach he could elude Nadja and transport himself to a metasexual dimension. In his arteries he could hear the undertow of his mortality. Each time he doubted his physical organism, so he returned to the idea of the portrait and its possible state of degeneracy. There was no way to disprove his intuitive feelings other than through direct consultation, and again he was tempted to confront the painting and read in it the story of his destiny. The dilemma raged in Dorian's nerves, and he resolved to go through the night's proceedings without the additional apprehension of realising his state of intrinsic deterioration. He decided he would face his mirror image on the morning after his marriage.

He had locked the door on Florentino and luxuriated in the

conspiratorial silence of his room. He was charging his energies. Prolonged initiations and harrowingly sustained ceremonies had taught him the dynamic necessary to visualise psychically the contents of the abyss. He dreaded a reversal taking place during the ceremony and that it would be a charred, shrunkenly reptilian old man's body which would face Florentino at the altar. There was the sound of a hollow rain flurry again. He could feel something dangerously gestating within him. There was a metamorphic thrust in his nerves. He could sense the collapse of an inner pivot, a deteriorating in his balancing of opposites: youth and age. Dorian needed to kill off the ageing body within him without any detriment to the youthful projection through which he lived. In that way his youth would prove incorruptible. His light would shine on like the unnaturally bright sunlight in a dream. His face would be gold, and his brainchild through Florentino would emulate his amazingly luminous features.

Movements inside the house told Dorian that it would soon be time to make final preparations. Under the disguise of heavy cloaks Dorian and Florentino would leave the house and join their small party at the deserted wharf. Already he imagined the scent of wet hemp and disturbed effluvia on the night waters. Something made him think of a giant key to an underwater city lying abandoned on the jetty. He would hold the key to one of the lost cities and claim his subaquatic kingdom.

They went out under a light rain, big, block-shaped clouds massing above the lagoon. The alleys were deserted, lights chinking out of closed shutters, an accordion squeezing notes from a raucously crowded café. Venice was like a dead city. The whole construct of historic architecture sitting on a ledge above the sea looked like a surreal artefact. Dorian and Florentino walked arm in arm through the wet streets. The Adriatic rushed to their nostrils. Under their black boating cloaks they were dressed in the ceremonial costumes of their marriage. They struck out a fast pace through the maze of alleys – a cat taking off into an electric trajectory lifted itself on to a courtyard wall. Its white bib glowed in the dark. They continued in silence through a complex of streets leading to the water. Dorian could hear the sea long before they reached it, the slow undulating lift of waters rising because they had nowhere else to go. And he knew they would be there. His little group was in under dark in the shelter of a warehouse. He knew they were all there and waiting: Mario and Paul, Umberto, Cesare and Jean-Yves, all in distinctive costumes under heavy cloaks. A retinue assembled to cross the waters, unaware of the full significance of the night's intended ceremony.

The two gondolas had been launched on the slipway. They were waiting on the largely undisturbed waters, lifting with the undertow, and Dorian could make out the flowers heaped at each prow and the emblematised cushions blazing in the stern. A light rain blew in but it was warm and tingled on the face. They boarded the two gondolas and put out into the night. There looked to be no one around. There were lights in windows all over the city, and excited laughter and music issuing from a courtyard near to the wharf. The landing-stage was a grid of undifferentiated spars with a red light twinkling at the end as the dark closed over them in their short passage out to San Michele. There was light on the water reflected from the sky, and in the distance shipping lights twinkling in solitary navigational passages through the cluster of islands. A red light and a green, lanterns slung on gunwales as the warm rain arrived and blew off in the inky marine night. Dorian had Mario and Florentino row him, while Umberto, Cesare and Jean-Yves followed in their wake. Dorian felt the night close over him cleanly, accedingly, absolutely. He looked round to ascertain that they were not being followed. It allowed him to be clear that if Nadja was on his trail then he must already be out on the island rather than in passage across the waters. He doubted that his enemy would be in waiting, but anxiety kept alerting him to that possibility.

They moved slowly and rhythmically towards their destination. There were no lights on the island, just a shipping one at the small jetty where boats tied up. They aimed for this fixed white light on the waters, hearing the lagoon open and close like the cutting of silk. Dorian sat huddled into himself, the occasional night breeze lifting strands of his hair. Whatever the situation, he never neglected his appearance, and his hand would periodically fly up to correct the confusion created by wind. They cut steadily through a wall of drizzling vapour. It was as if he could hear his heart beating in the waters. Its rhythm was a prominent bass-line intruding all along his veins. He felt himself once again to be the solitary magus in search of reversing his ruined destiny. To the others it was an excursion into peripheral psycho-sexual magic. Dorian imagined flipping over into the lagoon, and the hard, impacted shock of the waters swallowing him in a vortical grab to the core. It would be one way to break through the illusion of the possibilities awaiting him at death. And perhaps it really was as he had imagined it, a corridor with safety lights at the end of the regress, which would turn out to be the fluent mobility of messengers. He would be collected, but the real journey would begin then, with all the evaluation of experiential phases of his life.

They made the crossing almost too fast for Dorian. He had amplified each moment of the comforting rootlessness he had nurtured on the lagoon. He had felt as though his life could be washed out by the invading tides.

They tied up at the jetty and made their way in silence towards the chapel. There was no sound. An owl got its alarmingly nocturnal vocables out of a tree. Dorian led the way in a procession towards the building. Inside the chapel, he took off his boating cloak to reveal a velvet coat on which was embroidered the Aster Argos or silver star, representing the eye of Isis and her star, which is Sirius or Set. Dorian had chosen the symbol to emphasise the nature of Sirius as an immutable god beyond our solar system, one who embodies the undying characteristics of the phoenix. He had been shown the comparative indestructibility of his features and person, his immunity to illnesses, and he intended to concentrate his magical powers into furthering the deathlessness of his present state. By using the ophidian sexual current Dorian hoped to situate himself in a state of omniscient self-realisation. The delusional paranoia which made him think of himself as a god had from intermittent flashes of wondering built to the steady glow of a conviction. He had come to think of himself as gifted with properties to make himself dematerialise at will, and to rest from his pursuers in intervals of self-activated invisibility. He directed the others by his silent authority to the chapel. Inside they lit candles, and the place suddenly jumped alive in the contrast between light and shadow. It was like walking into a variant of the scene Dorian had imagined in his head all day. Things he had preconceived were now actual points of focus. Dorian had reached a level of mastery whereby he could contemplate any given sexual idea without emotion of any kind. He viewed his devotees with cold detachment as they set about preparing the altar for a marriage through psycho-sexual energies. What he conceived of mentally he intended to reproduce through the body. It was through this fusion, as Dorian conceived it, that human consciousness could be prepared to traffic with higher consciousness. And through that medium, if he operated the right frequency, he would avenge himself on Nadja and his company.

It was damp inside the chapel. The place smelt of disuse, deteriorative rot, and the remains of incense they had burnt there on previous nights. It felt as though a grey angel had wrapped itself over one of the rafters and was looking down with an oppressive overview of the proceedings. An angel sleeping out reality like a vagrant taking refuge from a freezing doorway. In Dorian's state of heightened nervous awareness anything seemed possible. It would not have surprised him to see Nadja lying on the altar naked, a lit candle extending vertically from his expanded mouth. And if there was rain outside it was beginning to argue its dialectic with stone. It was increasing to the steady beat of a hand-drum. Dorian had been using cocaine all day to heighten his sense of sexual stimulus. His attendants dressed the altar, while Florentino prepared himself to be the ceremonial bride.

Dorian's intention was to invoke certain spirits conjurable according to the Lesser Key of Solomon. According to the laws of goetic theurgy there were seventy-two spirits whom Solomon had shut up in a brass vessel and thrown into a deep lake. When the vessel was discovered by the Babylonians and the spirits were set free, they returned to their former places, and Dorian intended to summon a number of presences to his assistance. Because of the hour, Dorian would concentrate on the potent invocation of marquises amongst the seventy-two spirits, and having prepared the magic circle with the pentagram of Solomon drawn inside it, he sanctified the place with holy water and incense. Dorian's assistants sacrificed a black cock, and with the blood he drew the seal of Solomon on white parchment, to compel obedience and assumption of the human form when the spirit appeared. Dorian put on a white robe, the one he kept permanently at the chapel, and with his sceptre, sword and oil to anoint his temple and eyes, he prepared himself for conjuration with the brief prayer of lustration. He then invoked the assistance of Ancor, Amicar, Amides, Theodonias and Anitor, and concentrated his psychic energies towards ritualistic invocation.

With the place shut into intense silence, and with a veiled Florentino kneeling at the altar, Dorian felt integrated by the power he had assumed. He wanted to set in motion his own protection and the assassination of Nadja and his enemies. He began by invoking Marchosias, a powerful marquis who appears in the form of a wolf with griffin's wings, a whistling serpent's tail and fire streaming from his mouth. Dorian commanded the spirit to appear before the circle in human shape without any deformity or horror, and to give rational answers to his questions. The spirit was bound to fulfil his desires, and to pursue those ends with unconditional devotion. Dorian conjured Marchosias by the ineffable name Tetragrammaton Jehovah, by which the elements are mastered, the air made turbulent, the sea turned back, fire generated, and by which every celestial and infernal force is governed. Dorian affected a second and then a third conjuration, his mind lit with anticipation, the sense of expectation making the blood reverberate in his head. Flashes of light broke into his consciousness. The psychic energy in him burnt with the pressure of storm. He thought he was going to autocombust and be reduced to a cone of flaring ash. A blue and yellow flash jumped out of him, a seething energy ball of subatomic particles, and the hybrid bestial marquis materialised as a blinding image which cooled and steadied into human form. Dorian found himself confronting a tall, black-eyed, ferociously impacted form whose devotion to the operator was in direct proportion to the potential hostility he would project at an enemy. He was gloweringly, resolutely omnipotent. He had materialised from a quarter in which he was sovereign. Dorian stood in the circle and commanded. 'Come peaceably and affably, come visibly and without delay, manifest that which I desire, speak with a clear and intelligible voice, that I may understand you. I constrain you to answer truthfully.'

Dorian felt his body running by standing still. His whole system was on overdrive. He felt the absolute surety of his power. He confronted Marchosias without equivocation. Dorian named Nadja as his enemy, and as the shadow in his life who threatened him with murder. Dorian sensed the invisibility of his pact with the marquis. The others grouped at the altar were starting to engage in sexual contact, while Florentino remained passively kneeling in his own space, awaiting the ceremony. Their lives were going on independent of his magic liaison. Dorian asked for protection and for the destruction of his enemy. He enjoined Marchosias to have Nadja meet a violent end in the lagoon. He asked that his enemy's body should never be recovered, and that his name should disappear from the book of life. He questioned the marquis about circumstances surrounding his mortality, but because his questions wavered in authority and conviction, the marquis failed to reply. Dorian was conscious of the flaw in his assumed invincibility, and that a master in the order of domination would stand off from reciprocation with an exorcist who saw himself as fallible. Having acquired the promise of service from Marchosias, Dorian issued the marquis with a licence to depart, asking the spirit to withdraw quietly and without injury to anyone present, and to be willing to return and be exorcised by the sacred rites and magic.

Dorian continued to hold the circle and to recharge his psychic energies. After the next conjuration he would marry Florentino and advance his cause through psycho-sexual magic. Dorian could hear persistent rain drumming on the chapel roof. The night had settled to the heavy oppression of autumn rain. By candlelight Florentino looked the embodiment of androgynous beauty. More woman than man, and with his face made up, his scarlet lips hidden behind a net veil beaded with pearls, he owned to that re-created gender which is the more potent for its inclusion of both sexes into a compositely remade trans-creature. It was the defiance in re-creating the order of things that fascinated Dorian. All of Florentino's naïvety and innocence in terms of living experience were refuted by the psychological refutation of gender exchange.

Dorian resumed his magical authority by attempting to invoke a more benign marquis, Forneus, whose role is to cause men to be loved by their enemies as well as by their friends. Having requested Nadja's destruction, Dorian now hoped to find peace amongst his circle, a letting go of the pack whom he considered to be on his trail. Forneus's shape was that of a sea monster, and the gifts he conferred on the magician were those of the arts and good reputation, and tolerance amongst friends and enemies. Dorian prepared himself to conjure, concentrating his energies into a magnified focus on the image-power of his ritual. Once again the air was charged with electricity. He could feel his system tense, and his nerves threaten to shatter on overload. It was as if he were being torn along the divide between his right and left brain hemispheres. A force was moving in on him, and it was like the collision of two stars, an explosive gravitational field threatening to detonate his body in the circle. He saw a green and yellow light implode, experienced a cosmic rush of energy through his frontal lobes and psychically visualised the transformation of a sea-dragon with a whiplash appendage of needled tails into a green-eyed human, whose aura was like the wash of serene tides through a gully.

It was the sense of oceanic flux that helped Dorian find calm after the nerve-stripping intensity surrounding conjuration. There was an eloquence and a pervasive sense of equilibrium about this presence that infused the proceedings with calm. Forneus was disposed to the distribution of well-being, and to Dorian it seemed as if he were being given something ineffably sweet, a gift that heightened the moment like indefinable perfume picked out in a Paris street. Dorian asked for tolerance and the dropping of his name amongst enemies. But in asking, he was conscious of addressing an illusion.

As he had with Marchosias, so Dorian was aware of his own

imbalanced authority, and of the unintegrated components in himself which contributed to lack of direct exchange with the presence. Forneus proved difficult to command because his plane was abstract, and Dorian found himself momentarily inhibited in his functions. He adjured the marquis to bring him good repute in the world. He asked that his past misdemeanours should be forgotten and that the present company should be graced with Forneus's own attachment to the arts and rhetoric. Dorian did not detain Forneus long, his energies were over-stretched and he was quick to give the spirit licence to depart. He had mishandled the proceedings, but the sense of power he felt at his two conjurations was immense.

The rain was still coming on heavily outside. Dorian moved out of the circle and took up his place at Florentino's side. He was going to marry him in the presence of his four assistants, and consummate that love in the circle. And all the time he was becoming increasingly obsessed about the possible state of his portrait and what it would tell him about his future. He found himself desperate to live out of defiance to the natural orders of the universe. He would make himself impermeable to everyone and everything. And to subvert heterodoxy he had had made for Florentino a silver ring with the seal of Zepar on it, a duke who inflamed women with a libidinous passion for men, and who turned them into nymphomaniacs who culti-vated every form of excess to appease their pleasure. Florentino would never know of the potency behind this hermetic symbol. He would read into it no more than a wedding-ring, and as Dorian slipped it on to the young man's finger, so he medi-tated on the sacrilege entailed by the act. Florentino kissed him lightly, and it was for Dorian like the retrieval of a sensation he had known a long time ago before his life had radically evolved according to the principles of the left-handed world. He thought of the lacerating kisses he had exchanged with Harry, and the hook of mutual loathing on which their love had hung. Those kisses had drawn blood and tasted of barbed wire.

Florentino offered love with the submissiveness of a woman. He wanted to be consumed by Dorian: he needed to live in his shadow. And Dorian was conscious for a moment of how little of him Florentino would ever have. His own mind was a chaotic assemblage of possible flights into exile, recriminations of his enemies, and alertness to the possibilities of his death. He was marrying an innocence that would be crushed under his heel. And now as the consummation of his profane rite, Dorian offered Florentino's body to the altar. He joined him in a union endorsed by his transvestite disciples. With the rain doubling its intensity and the night rubbing against the walls like a panther, they engaged in the orgiastic excesses of sexual magic. For Dorian sex was the orchestrating principle of the rites, the tangent on which he would lose consciousness of his identity.

Dorian moved from partner to partner, anxious to break down all physical boundaries, and to have no sense of individuated being. He lost himself in a body-dance of scorching pleasure. He felt he was being tossed on a series of bull's horns from one body to another. And when he lay exhausted, wrapped in the red altar-cloth, there was light chinking into the chapel, a blue leakage filtering through high windows to expose their twisted bodies. Dorian knew they should be gone soon. He wanted to get back to the city before the day broke. He feared the light finding him and his party out. He hurried everyone into their clothes, and they all draped boating cloaks over their exotic dress.

They shambled out of the chapel under a blue-black sky, the rain smoking off, lights twinkling on the horizon. Dorian's party were drugged, sleep-drenched, almost somnambulistic in their exhaustion. They stumbled towards the quay, where the two gondolas could be made out, lifting slightly on the heavy waters. To Dorian the return would be a bitter one, no matter that he had asserted his magical prowess as a way of shaping his destiny. He looked disconsolately at the lagoon, the prospect of the return crossing filling him with dread. He was making a transition from the extraordinary to the ordinary, he was going back to be reassimilated by life. When they reached the jetty and he lowered himself into the craft, his hand felt the blade of a knife stood upright through a sheet of paper. He extracted the blade and held the paper up to his eyes, and read the words, I WILL KILL YOU – NADJA.

 *Chapter 6*

WHEN Harry looked up from his book and his wife's familiar features swam into view, he felt momentarily bilocated. In drifting out he had imagined himself back in Paris in the apartment he had shared with Dorian. In his lapse into unconsciousness he was eyeing a fruit-bowl on the table when a tarantula put out its black hairy legs from under a peach. Harry had been transfixed by fear, he was sure that the portentous creature was about to kill him, when Dorian's hand had closed over it like an impacted cage.

Harry blinked his eyes and the room righted itself. His Mayfair house had not changed in his absence. He was sitting in his library with its olive-stained wainscot of oak, its cream-coloured frieze and raised plaster-work ceiling, the brickdust-coloured felt carpet strewn with silk Persian rugs. Some large blue china jars were packed with seasonally yellow chrysanthemums. Harry felt the reassuring vibration of London traffic settle around the house like an ambient backdrop. It was somehow a part of his nerves, this huge motory thrust of a capital with its hundreds of cars connecting along points, all directed by the dictates of individual lives. He could not imagine waking or sleeping without the reassurance of that simmering vibrato. Sometimes it reminded him of the baritone wash of a sea pushing in and out of a hollow cave.

Harry's wife was reading a novel, her straw-coloured hair falling across one side of her face and cut short on the other. The green silk dress she was wearing exposed her silk-stockinged legs. Harry looked at her without her being able to see he was looking. He liked the subtle psychological advantage this scrutiny afforded, and sustained the tension knowing that at some point it would break and her washed-out blue eyes would look inquiringly at his in the hope he would speak.

He was amazed at the transformation in Victoria since the period he had spent in Paris with Dorian. What he had anticipated would provoke a stony and inveterately moral hostility in a woman with whom he had never been truly intimate, had set up quite the opposite reaction. She had proved to be without reproach for his sexual relations with Dorian, and at first it was he who found it difficult to be honest about preferences for which she manifested a profound understanding. He had begun with the assumption that she was extracting information in order to present watertight divorce proceedings, and was simulating love in order to achieve her ends. Life with Dorian had placed Harry in a world of emotional distortion, where manipulation and deception were part of the natural vocabulary. Adjusting to an existence in which speech and intentions were directed towards honest impulses was hardest of all, and Harry realised how the hermetic, nocturnal world had succeeded in reversing his natural instincts. He had been twisted out of his centre. Not only had Vicky given him psychological support, but her new sense of being a sexual woman, in terms of expressing a more liberated femininity, had shown itself through the clothes she wore, the books she read and the opinions she voiced. She had radically changed in his years of aberrant estrangement in Paris. He was both frightened of her and attracted to her assertive feminine mystique. It was not so much that she set out to seduce him as to show him her erotic potential as a woman. In the past she had fallen in love regularly but her sexuality had been reserved, and the externalisation of it gauche, flirtatious but altogether contained. Harry's sexual relations with his wife had been intermittent and unsatisfactory, and almost non-existent after his meeting with Dorian. His impulse to visit her locked bedroom had left him. He had felt little affection in the opposite sex for what he had come so easily to imitate in himself. It was he who had worn perfume and taken to pronouncing feminine accoutrements in his person. He had dispensed with the need for women by exaggerating that gender role in himself. And Vicky had retreated into what perhaps she had assumed was her role, that of the passive woman who was fortunate to have secured a good marriage. Someone who must maintain her dignity by proving uncomplaining, and who would settle into a life of neglect, and an endless round of social activity.

Looking into her forget-me-not blue eyes, as she stared up from her book into the light streaming through the high window, Harry felt the beginnings of a love for a woman he had consigned to perpetual neglect. There was a sympathy in her that longed to find union with a lover. She had perhaps surprised herself by the depths of her reserves of compassion and understanding. She had discovered so much in herself that she was unable to share, and as Harry looked at her discreetly, he felt he could forgive her completely for the affair that had so changed her life in his absence. They had both learnt a different set of emotions in their lives spent apart. And while his initial response had been to write her out of his name for her infidelities, he had learnt to consider how much more difficult it must be for a woman to forgive her husband a relationship with another man that it was for him to forgive her for an affair to which she had been driven. His first impulse was to avenge himself in the manner that Dorian meted out destruction on lovers who crossed him. He had proved intolerable company for a month, his mind preoccupied with his bruised ego, his nerves simmering with unresolved chaos. He had been waiting his time to rip into her in a scene calculated to bring an instant end to their marriage, when one afternoon he had discovered one of the letters Vicky had sent him in Paris. In it was expressed a sensitivity to his feelings and a generosity of emotion towards his extreme situation that persuaded him to rethink his intended strategy. His social position was irretrievably ruined, his emotions had been scorched and holed by Dorian, and he had found himself without friends. He had no intention of dipping into his homosexual past and retrieving contact with a world of nocturnal outlaws who eagerly swam to the surface of the deep at the first glitter of money. All those cosmetic faces would be in his street again, they would appear when he least expected them, making their insistent demands. Harry could not take that all over again. The scene in Paris had exhausted him. He had put his head into the lion's mouth and emerged enervated. He had suddenly realised that the possibilities of a future lay at his feet, and that the person whom he had always abstracted and ruled out of his intimate life was the one who could give him back the stability and self-confidence he needed to face the future.

He had kept Vicky as a shadow in his life, an unrealised woman who had jolted him into an awareness of his angularity each time they were together. She had become to him like a dead star receding in space. And then one afternoon, after they had each spoken tentatively about their missing time, he had felt an increasing sexual attraction towards her. Perhaps it was the pencil-line seams in her silk stockings and the way her skirt had ridden up to reveal the curve of her thighs, and the way it had happened involuntarily, which had put a tense glow in his abdomen. He had not felt sexual excitement of this nature since his first meeting with Dorian. He felt as if the dark sun that had previously occupied his unconscious was no longer in ascension, and that a new light was flooding his sexual energies. But he had waited and not acted on his immediate impulses.

It was when Vicky had gone to her room in the evening to change that he had found himself compelled to follow her upstairs. He had stood outside her bedroom door and listened to the crackle of her zip, and the concertina rustle of her dress as it fell to the floor. Harry knew she was standing in a pool of black silk and that it was the time for him to enter the room. Vicky did not register any surprise, as though she had expected this to happen, her standing there in her black suspenders and the almost lilac translucency of her silk stockings, her bottom reflected back at him from the opposite mirror, while Harry just stared at her with incandescent intensity. They had come together without saying a word and he had entered her forcefully, his whole life blanking out as the sexual urgency rushed into his genitals. Their love-making had been prolonged and repeated, their animal passion finding a surprise reciprocity. All the years of mutually repressed hostility were savagely buried by their ferocious orgasmic release.

In the aftermath and afterglow of sex a sympathy had established itself between them, so that they lay together in the process of healing. They lay in each other's arms without noticing that the night had built up outside to a solid blue-black cube; and they never spoke a word. Feelings had dispensed with speech, and Harry had feared to disengage his body from the woman in whom he had found such refuge and pleasure. They had each anticipated that a single word would crack the spell. What they had experienced was a form of psychic osmosis, and it accounted for the genuine sympathy Harry felt for Vicky as he looked at her eyes waver between reading and reflection. He suddenly wanted to know this woman, and on some tangent enter into the pain and joy that comprised her life. The complex, individual unit that was Vicky, with stardust travelling through her veins, and somewhere the DNA blueprint of her equally individual death showing up on the monitor. It was a sensation he had not known before, and one that transmitted ambivalent associations of pain and compassion. Harry suddenly imagined Vicky dead, and experienced his own terrifying sense of isolation at the prospect. He wanted to tell her of his portentous inner dialogue, but he jammed back on himself and said nothing.

It was Vicky who spoke first. She must have sensed the drift of Harry's thought, for she looked direct into his eyes and said, 'I should tell you about myself. I should tell you what happened. We are both in the dark, and perhaps it is easier for me to talk. I have fewer inhibitions than you.' And again she looked direct into Harry's eyes.

He was momentarily disarmed. But before he could take up with any reservations, Vicky threw her eyes down at the floor and said, 'I had to do it. I was so lonely when you left without warning. And of course, I knew you had gone to join Dorian. You did not even leave me a note. At the time I hated you. It took a relationship with another man for me to discover my love for you. It was a necessary experience. Through it I discovered my sexuality. In the past our marriage was ruled by repression and all manner of compromise. You cannot imagine what I suffered, and what women suffer. There appeared no way out. I used to lie in bed at night contemplating ways which would lead to a divorce. It became my obsessive fantasy. How to free myself of bonds I could not be without. I knew you did not desire me sexually, but at the same time it seemed that we had never had the chance to come together. Nor did I know what I was supposed to do, or what role was expected of me. I had no idea whether I was supposed to seduce you or you me. I had no experience. How could I have known what to do? My parents brought me up with no knowledge of sex.

'It must have been about the time you went away that I met Benjamin, at one of those lifeless functions I was expected to attend. His ideas were so shockingly controversial, so intelligently outspoken, that I was compelled to listen. And each time he spoke, he would run his eyes over my body, as though he was undressing me. At first I was outraged and wanted to storm out of the room. I had never been treated in this way, but his manner, which at first I had rejected, began slowly to win me. I was being swallowed by the enemy. I was frightened of the compulsion I felt for this man. I knew he had infiltrated his way into me and could do with me as he wished. If I tell you things that hurt you, it is because we must establish a truth between us.'

Harry was resting his head on one arm, and Vicky could see him tensing, as though his pride was irreparably affronted, but she knew she had to continue.

'Anyhow, we made a secret rendezvous to meet that next day. I never knew where you were, and so it was easy to arrange these meetings. I amazed myself by giving in the first time. You had never, Harry, shown me sexual love or passion, and so this was a new experience, and it changed me. It taught me that women too could know sexual pleasure and enjoy it as just that without any deep complications. I don't believe in promiscuity, for I know you will think of it in those terms. What I suppose I discovered was the body. I had been ashamed of it until Benjamin taught me its sensuality and sensitivity. Learning to accept it was like discovering how to play a musical instrument. I had lived without my body. And so I kept on going back for more. Sex, ideas, a whole new code of living. It seemed to me that I had always been dead, and that I was only now beginning to discover myself. There were so many aspects of life for which I lacked knowledge. At first I wanted to experience everything for the first time. I was like a child. I dared to think that life, after all, was good. I had never entertained that thought before. I had always seen it as something to endure. A process one got through. But I want you to believe this, I never once envisaged giving myself totally to Benjamin, I was excited by his intellect and his nonconformity and the body language he explored, but I never loved him. I needed him as an antidote to my feelings of loneliness and rejection. He became everything to me in a bad time except the man I loved. And when I was with him I used to wonder where you were, and my hatred for Dorian would force me to contract my fist and want to beat it on the wall.

'Then my emotions went the opposite way. I began to blame myself. I said to myself that if I had offered more as a wife you would never have gone off with a man. I saw in myself every justification for a man to judge me as a failure. I had lost love and had to learn from a stranger how I might have pleased that man. I was having to live my life backwards. I never invited Benjamin to this house, this lonely building where I was in truth waiting for you. We continued to meet in hotels. I suppose I liked the anonymity and excitement of it, and he was already committed in various ways at first, although he wanted to give up everything for me. But as I said, Harry, I never loved him. And I am not saying this to soften the blow for you. I had discovered animal passion for a body. And I was learning from Benjamin's flagrant iconoclasm in respect of gender. He taught me that women were men's equal, and should within a harmonious relationship be able to express themselves without a sense of inferiority.

'These were big things for me to swallow. I am still learning to assimilate most of what I was taught. There are things I have adopted, and others that it will take a long time to evaluate. At one time I did not know who I was, the changes were too huge and too many. I thought I had been destroyed. And when your letters began to arrive from Paris, I knew that you were searching for a lifeline. You had always prevented me showing the love I felt for you, and I began by thinking that if you trusted me enough to write to me, at a time when you were living with Dorian, then I must at least be a friend to you. I used to lie awake at night thinking perhaps you recognised unconsciously that I loved you. And then months would go by and I would receive no letter from you. I would write to the post office number you gave me, and wait on each post. And of course I would ask myself if I was in love with an illusion, and if I was constructing a fantasy to compensate for the absence of real love in my life. I went through these various swings of mood, oscillating between belief in myself and the complete absence of it. I ask you not to be hard on me. I have suffered deeply. I stayed with you as a sort of empathy. And I wish you would tell me one day – one day – what it is like to live with and love a man. Is Dorian as bad as I imagine? I still hate him with a fury. But I do not believe he has destroyed us. There is nothing that cannot be rebuilt.'

Vicky stopped talking. The silence settled again, and she sat there realising that in a short space of time she had given voice to all her most central preoccupations for the past four years. She had risked everything by her disclosures, but she had lacked choice in the matter. The volume of it was so much bigger than she was that it had spoken for her. She had listened to herself with the same surprise Harry must have inwardly expressed at her confession. She could feel the balance being restored between them, and also Harry's sudden immersion in himself as the selective process began.

'It is almost impossible for me,' he said, 'to begin. What I have known in Paris, the world into which Dorian so unprotestingly led me, is a world so terrible and so different from anything that you have experienced, that I wonder if I shouldn't spare you the details. What shall I tell you and what conceal?'

'Tell me everything,' Vicky said. 'Don't spare me. What you have experienced can hardly be worse than what I have imagined about you. Anything would be a release from pain.'

'I will try,' said Harry, 'impossible as it may seem. I have come to look with horror on my past. I view it with repugnance and revulsion, and yet only a short time ago I was engaging in a sexual world which should have killed me, so extreme were its practices. Even to take you there in the imagination will be an immensely painful journey. Coming back to conventional life after what I have been through is like returning to another planet.

'When I first met Dorian, it confirmed my homosexual propensities. I suppose most of my sexual relations had been with men. I had never wanted to acknowledge it. And when I met you I carried on living in the same way under the screen of marriage. I never attempted to make the adjustment. I just viewed our relationship as one of convenience. I suspected that as long as I was married, no one would make too many inquiries into my private life. It seemed the perfect social cover. A chance for me to experiment with my inclinations. And when I met Dorian I discovered in him not only a lover but a guide to self-debasement. We were too extravagant, and London too small. It came to be dangerous. Dorian introduced me to a nocturnal milieu. I have no means of justifying my conduct, none at all, only that the whole thing asserted such a fascination over me that I was compelled to risk arrest again and again.'

'And you used to come home to this house afterwards?' Vicky tentatively inquired. 'You didn't think of sparing my feelings?'

'On the contrary,' said Harry, 'and you have asked me to be totally honest – my disrespect for you at the time, for marriage, for convention, heightened the pleasure I got from these nocturnal rampages. It was something I was working through. At the time I could not see it, could not locate my lack of self-esteem as the source.'

'It is hard for a woman to understand the brutality of this sexual quest,' Vicky said quietly.

'I would say impossible,' replied Harry in a voice of quiet self-reflection. 'It is a world of bodies in which love is absent. Numbers instead of feelings, as Dorian expressed it. No one who has not passed through that fire could understand the disdain with which people are used and rejected.

'And it got worse in Paris. Dorian grew more and more desperate to live in the moment. Our own relationship started to fall apart. And once the deterioration set in, there was no going back on it. I found myself torn in two. A part of me wanted to be forgiven and return to you, and the other part of me wanted to heal Dorian and love him again. He was pursuing occult studies and was steeped in black magic. The aura in the apartment grew to be so dark that I developed asthma and all manner of psychosomatic illnesses.

'Every day I looked clearly at my death. I did not assume I had the right to live. Everything around me was in ruins. I expected the law to arrive at any moment and arrest us. But through a system of magic Dorian had established a code of self-protection. It is not something I understand, but it works for him. Although we were known for our habits, we were never apprehended by the law. I suppose that is why I am here with you now and not in a cell. I sometimes find myself savouring the moment, extending it sweetly, biting on it as if I had never valued freedom before.

'My crimes,' Harry continued, 'were against myself and you. I went deep into self-punishment. I was associating with a bad lot. There was the poet Paul Verlaine and his crowd, but worse than that were the clubs I visited. Dorian introduced me to this world, and I pursued it with fascination and sexual hunger. Do you really want me to go on?'

Harry looked across at Vicky's strained features. Her eyes were still luminous with compassion, although he could see how the pain was pinching her on the inside. He half expected her to burst into tears.

'Go on,' she said. 'I can follow it to the end.'

'When I tell you these things,' said Harry, 'it seems as though someone else has lived through the ordeal. I gave up most of the things which had formed a big part of my life. I no longer read, socialised, engaged in conversation or hunted out antiques. I gave up visiting the theatre. I gave up doing everything. Our apartment was rarely open to the day. It was heavy with perfume, smoke and the preternatural aura surrounding Dorian's person. I would hear liturgical imprecations coming from his room as the evening advanced. Jinxed things would happen. All the lights would fuse, a book would open itself of its own accord, the apartment bell would ring and there would be no-body there. And one day there was, and standing there was a headless man in a black suit and white shirt. It was then that I knew I had to leave. I was on the way to a breakdown. Things reached a climax when Dorian presented himself as the sacrificial messiah at a club and was hoisted on to a cross and savaged.

'I boarded the first train out of Paris the next morning and checked into a Swiss sanatorium. It was from there that you first started to receive my letters regularly. You became my only hope on an impossible horizon. I did not yet dare to believe that love could exist between us, I was too emotionally scarred at the time, but you were like a door left open, through which the light shone. Getting rid of the past was like taking out stitches. My mind was saturated with Dorian. When the clear mountain air shone through my window, it purified me. And at night the stars continued with that dialectic of light. I sat on my chair at the window, denied alcohol, my hands shaking, my nerves shot through with terror. All of my years in Paris re-turned to me like a film. Only there were increasing jumps of light between the dark incidents. It was of course a process of self-evaluation. I hated myself and had to find a way to live again. Everything had collapsed. . . . It amazes me that you can listen to this confession.'

'What you are telling me is of course worse than anything I could have imagined,' said Vicky. 'But I have learnt from this ordeal that our worst fears have their basis in reality. All I know is that we cannot reverse the action, and that as a woman I have taken on what most would find unacceptable. Absolutely intolerable. I will simply say I understand desperation.'

'How could I have imagined whom I had married,' said Harry. 'I saw you as a woman tied to your social class. Nothing more than that. Someone conditioned by a particular education and a set of values which wouldn't change in the course of a life-time. I thought you would be unquestioning about everything, so I would live an independent existence and do as I wished. And that is what happened. I made myself available to Dorian because I lived as though I was single. The idea of my being married never occurred to either of us. It seemed the least obstructive of obstacles. So I destroyed all balance in my life. It may take me a year, five years or ten to recover. Can you really accept that? Can you live through my rehabilitation?'

'Love will cure a lot of things,' said Vicky. 'I can wait for as long as that process takes. But you still haven't told me about Dorian. I mean the real person. Who is he?'

'I don't really know,' said Harry. 'He is the ultimate enigma. I am not even sure if he is human. He is preternaturally evil. Nothing touches him. Not even the little things in life. He never gets ill. He is unable to break out of his role. He suffers in it. I am not saying this mitigates his actions, but it has something to do with it. Nor am I arguing a case for evil, but this is Dorian's destiny, it is his individuated role. He has attracted a source and it works through him. What is right and what is wrong surely depends on the control or lack of it we assert over our actions. I don't know if Dorian has that mediating power of control. And there is, you know, the enigma of the portrait. I saw it a long time ago, when Basil Hallward was working on it. Dorian has changed very little since that portrait was painted, or perhaps more than that, he has become the embodiment of the painting. There is a mystery behind this painting which he won't ever discuss. He claims he left the painting here in London, but I know it is still in his possession. He guards it, and perhaps because it contains the secret of his death. That is my particular theory.'

'But why is he left to live in this manner?' said Vicky. 'Surely he is wanted by the law? I fail to understand.'

'Sometimes I do not even think he is real,' said Harry. 'Later on, after our relationship had ended, I used to imagine that if I touched him he would prove invisible. There is too much charge surrounding him. It is like an electric storm. There were times when he would stay in his room for a week at a time. He would be engaged in secret rites. I would find black hens in the refrigerator. And the things he would eat – peacocks, birds of paradise, lions, tigers and elephant steaks. He acquired the rarest of gourmet foods, delicacies that cost a fortune and which were procured through illicit sources. He contrived it so that he knew almost no normal company. He mixed only with the underworld. It was a trait that had begun in London. He despised the normal and could only relate to the weird. For years these people were my only contacts too. I adjusted to Dorian's milieu, even if I found it only superficially attractive.'

'Are you telling me the whole truth?' questioned Vicky.

'There are things I would rather spare you,' Harry replied. 'Like the nature of what I believe his crimes to be. There are so many rumours, it is impossible to distinguish truth from lies.'

'And if you were called upon to testify,' said Vicky, 'would you disclose what you know?'

Harry remained silent for a long time, took a deep breath, and said finally, 'No, I would not. I would not say a word. But if you think this is a confirmation of my love for him, you are wrong. I would say nothing because he has had to live through the experience of it all. I would not wish that journey, nor – am I sure – would you. I come back again to the notion of the why of individual experience. You may argue that Dorian has voluntarily made himself a receptor for evil, but it is more complex than that. In a way he has been appointed. This is his role.'

Harry took a brief glance at the book-wedged shelves thrusting up to the ceiling. A predominantly grey sky had opened out like a fan to reveal big lakes of peacock-blue and green. He watched Vicky rearrange her legs like two silk flowers on seamed stems. She smoothed down the hem of her skirt, flattened it, and appeared to be editing her thoughts before she looked up and said, 'It's not that I think you love me less. Your pain is that your sexuality is divided. You fear to let anyone down, Harry, so you oscillate between the two sexes. You end up injuring both, while intending to harm neither. I am not asking you to eliminate your attraction to men, I am wanting you to integrate it. What is important is that you should love me as you are. It is going to be hard to get Dorian out of your system. I personally think he is evil. Wilfully and voluntarily. And this is my one condition: that you never meet him or write to him again. Not in any circumstances. I would forgive you everything but that. Never ask me to do so.'

Harry bit into his memories, which were like a sharp orange. Even though Dorian had come close to destroying him, there were shared experiences he could never let go. Dorian continued to jump in and out of his consciousness, as though his mind were an open window. At one time he would have heard the crash of the glass, but now the register was a low, subdued one. He had established distance on his experience. And while Harry nurtured immediate resentment at Vicky's unnegotiable stipulation, he realised it was the homoerotic in him that continued to be indirectly loyal to Dorian. He was conscious it was not something he could immediately erase.

'I think I can promise you that,' Harry said. 'But sometimes, you know, there's a finale to these things, a contact is made at the end, because there has to be some sort of inner resolution to conflict. If for instance Dorian were to die, or needed to see me to confess, or I to him in an extreme state, would you deny me that right? Sometimes these things can be of huge importance.'

'Don't try to persuade me to retract on my condition,' said Vicky. 'These are things I cannot immediately answer. Any woman would hate this man for stealing her husband. I think I have shown extraordinary tolerance already.'

'You have,' said Harry. 'But it's just that I have a premonition, a sense of impending disaster in the air. I can't account for it. Something is going to happen to Dorian soon. I know he has moved to Venice, and I imagine he is still there.'

'I don't want to know where he is, Harry,' Vicky interpolated.

'But hear me out. These things carry cosmic significance. I ask myself if Dorian is capable of dying. That is a human action, and perhaps part of his great pain is that he is denied that right. He once told me that all his suicide attempts had failed, even when he had used the most stringent of poisons, arsenic. I suppose I can't unconsciously disconnect. The process is still working through me, even if I am no longer a part of it. That is why I continue to feel these things. I know there is a huge crisis building. It could break cover at any time. I know he is there. It is not a dialogue we share, it is more a series of received messages on my part, and what I assume to be transmitted impulses on his. Maybe it is just something in the air.'

'I cannot stop you telepathically communicating with Dorian,' said Vicky. 'But I wish I could stamp out even that. I would like to silence him totally. Of course I would.'

'I suppose that is the sadness and isolation of the individual,' said Harry. 'We can't get inside someone to alter the mechanism of their thinking. Everything we would like to change is unchangeable. But that is the part of individual sanctity. If we went into somebody too far, we would cease to have any boundaries. We would re-create them in ways which may be intolerable to them.'

'I don't care if Dorian is dying,' said Vicky, 'you are not going to see him. Not in any circumstances.'

At last Harry put down the book which he had been keeping open on his lap. In speaking about Dorian, he was conscious of how much of him there was in his head. He had been unloading the man like a series of composite building blocks. And in speaking about him, he had not only been re-creating him but discovering factors he did not know. It was another Dorian he mentally confronted, one who had gained additional dimensions in the course of his discussion with Vicky. He saw Dorian again walking through the apartment after days spent locked away in magical study. There were pentagrams splashed on his gown and over his body. His eyes were black with fatigue. There was an aura around him that stood out like the radial points of a star. He would passively accept Dorian's deranged and estranged behaviour. He would tolerate the cognoscenti when they called. The usual transvestite hangers-on, who entertained Dorian with stories of their clients, and who engaged in constant salacious repartee. For a moment he was back there, before he abruptly relocated himself in the present.

Harry placed a hand in Vicky's. There was suddenly an aliveness in their touch, like that of two small sympathetic creatures who had come together, tingling with expectation. They let their hands find a comfortable pivot, a resting-point from the world, and a bonding axis on which their lives depended. For a moment Harry felt loved, and as his usual feelings of insecurity overtook him again, he marvelled at Vicky's ability to trust. It was she who had every reason to express reservations about the future of their relationship. It was Vicky who had been left, but Harry could observe how her inner strength gave her the confidence to trust in love again. It was a capacity he lacked. He knew it accounted for the desperation with which he cut rapidly from one sex to the other. No one and nothing seemed to afford him the forgetting for which he longed. He was lacking a centre, and if he had lacked one before he met Dorian, their life together had fragmented the little stability he had once had. His core was in fission.

They sat together in silence. The city pushed at the library windows, the tension vibrating in the glass. It was pressure spreading and falling like rain. All those ambient decibels transmitted through the air-waves. To Harry it always seemed as if the universe were about to jump inside. And when they started to talk again, they discussed smaller things, like the books they were reading, things to be done in the house, the seasons as they drifted in and out of memory. And more tangible dilemmas, like health, Vicky's stubbornly recurrent migraines, and Harry's kidney problems, occasioned by the excess of alcohol he had consumed in Paris. Vicky's migraines would require further consultation in the effort to locate the stress-trigger that sent blindingly painful shooting stars searing behind her eyes. If Vicky had deepened during their years of separation, then Harry could see how her femininity was enhanced as a consequence of her arriving within herself. She had grown into a woman without perhaps ever intending to be that. The germinal person he had known was still there, but the enhanced aspects were psychic factors that had come into being independent of him.

'It may be, Harry,' said Vicky, 'that you will offer me the love that you would prefer to give a man, but which in me will find a compromise. I can accept that, providing you are true to me. What I do not want is falsity. Yet I believe in time you will love me as a woman. Have we not already begun that process? We have found a physical union that we have never known before. I have hope. I would not be here for you if I did not.'

Harry reflected deeply on her words. Vicky had touched the source within him to which he had hardly dared own. Had he not, he considered, always treated Vicky with emotional neutrality which denied her existence as a woman? He sensed the broken mirror in himself, the fragments reflecting his inner chaos, and the whole unresolved dilemma of his sexual orientation. He wanted to love this woman and renounce his past, but he needed to feel it and to experience it without a sense of intellectual detachment placing him back in the field of compromise. Again he felt a growing sexual need for Vicky, a fire that ran like a hot vine from his stomach to his genitals. He felt the nerves catch in a growing blaze. The urgency in him must have communicated itself to her, for Vicky brought her chair closer and her lips opened in a scarlet oval, inviting and expecting his kiss, and then were on his like a trembling flower. They tasted of violets, and Harry brought his own instructive force to them, teasing at first, then finding a centre and injecting his tongue to carry the storm of his passion. The point of his tongue was aimed at Vicky's intangible core. If only he could have located her like a bee exploring a flower's corolla. He would have liked to extend that pointed tip fraction by fraction to meet with her soul. And perhaps then, he reflected, he would be convinced of the truth of her identity.

Vicky came and sat on his lap, and reflexively Harry drew back, remembering that she must have learnt this method of seduction from her affair with Benjamin, but he relaxed and surrendered to the intimacy of the move, his body hardening beneath her compliant sexuality. All of the mystery of her sex was pivoted on his arousal. When he looked over her shoulder and up and out through the high windows, he could see a uniformly clear sky flooding into blue. It was no longer patchy but convexly, transparently delphinium blue. He gave himself up completely to Vicky's caresses, and for the time there was a big empty space in his head. Dorian had gone away. He had an image of him running along an alley, his hair dyed red, death in his eyes, and then Harry was carrying Vicky upstairs towards a room in which they would find oblivion through love.

Chapter 7

FLORENTINO sat in a courtyard and the sunlight poured through the heavy, spatulate fig leaves. He squatted in the diffused shade, his red and white striped matelot's shirt bottled into tight jeans. He was waiting for Mario to arrive, waiting for a knock at the door. He had been in hiding from Dorian for the past week, concealed in a friend's house in a tangle of wharfside courtyards and attempting to piece together bit by bit the various threads of his suspicions about Dorian. He was no longer able to tolerate Dorian's unpredictable mood-swings, his increasingly secret hours, and the dark that seemed to lead from him as a malevolent emanation.

Florentino's naïvety and trust had been broken. His initial fascination with a world of values so different from his own had declined, and the spell broken, he had begun in the cold sobering aftermath to assess the terror of his situation. What he had thought in Dorian to be simply a difference, an exaggeration of extreme characteristics that excited Florentino's love of transvestism and ritual, had changed from a dangerous infatuation to a life-threatening relationship. Florentino feared for his life. Return or stay, he knew that Dorian's recriminations would be devastatingly revengeful. He had made the break and he was determined not to be drawn back into Dorian's life. Whatever possessions he had, the extravagant wardrobe of clothes which had been given him, and all the aesthetically chosen gifts of rings, perfumes and hand-made shoes, he had left behind without any compunction. The instinctual need to exorcise Dorian from every aspect of his life had grown into an urgent compulsion. He knew he could walk away from everything but the memories. They would pursue him all of his life, consciously and unconsciously, for he had been bitten intransigently by his antagonist.

He sat on a packing-crate positioned beneath a tree and placed his bare feet on the cool stone. Someone was hammering in a shipping-yard nearby, the dull staccato reverberations of metal on metal punching holes in the air. He could smell the tide sliding through the stagnant lagoon. There was a tang of hawsers, chains, tar, dacron rope, flotsam nosing on inert pools, and a sound that was always there, untranslatably evanescent but which reminded him of a piano being played under water. It was the whole marine ethos in which he had grown up, the sea-roads leading out from the aquamarine lagoon to peninsulas around the world. In his childhood the sea had come to represent visions of sun-soaked beaches, sailors marooned in colonies on desert islands, red hibiscus flowers bursting out of the shore, and great staggering skies building high over shorelines with radiant scintillas of stars receding into the back of infinity. He had created his own universe of fantastic visions, and always the sea had flowed through it, its blue arm expanding boundaries, pushing to limitless frontiers with the expansive monotony of surf. He would close his eyes and float out on the current, lie on his back and drift all the way to America. He had hung around water from his childhood, fascinated by jetties, landing-bays, harbours, sailors and tourist arrivals. He did not know what any of its associations represented, only that they meant something he could not properly explain, a sort of longing from which he never wished to be separated. He was stuck on the idea of summer, the sexual excitement of tourists crowding along the Lido, the citric tang of a cologne he could not identify, dispersing in strains on the air, and the whole colour-saturated, humid, lazy aura that hung over his city.

Florentino's train of thought was broken by a low rap on the wooden door, repeated three times as was the prearranged signal.

He got up from his position under the fig tree and moved tentatively towards the door. Mario's voice was calling his name in undertones, urgent, nervous, importunate. Florentino lifted the heavy double bolts on the gate and Mario was there, his dark hair gelled back, his thin torso framed in a blue denim shirt. There was somebody else with him, and Mario was quick to reassure Florentino that his friend had important things to tell him about Dorian.

Florentino opened the door and the two young men quickly stepped into the closed courtyard. Florentino was immediately struck by Mario's tall companion. His blond hair and natural androgyny made him stand out as not belonging anywhere. Far more than the predictable transvestites, with whom Florentino associated at bars, this creature, whom Mario introduced as Nadja, struck an immediate chill into Florentino. He knew at once it was the person stalking Dorian. Nadja's eyes were made up with mascara and eye-liner, and he wore a black satin shirt with light cotton pants. But underneath Nadja's overt femininity Florentino could sense a dominant masculinity, the repressed rage of male integrants that had been denied assimilation by Nadja's split gender. Florentino had little doubt that Nadja meant every threat he had delivered to Dorian. He was suspicious of this uninvited caller and sniffed hostility, but Mario was there to reassure him, and he quickly found himself won over by Nadja's smile and the intimate confidentiality of his speech. But at the same time he continued to be afraid and to view Nadja with suspicion.

The three of them sat down in the shade, and Florentino brought out a bottle of wine and glasses. A siren wailed spook-ily across the waters, and they could hear a *vaporetto* churn a white swathe through the green channel.

'This is Nadja,' said Mario. 'He wants to talk to you about Dorian and the danger we could all be in if he lets loose his energies on us. I never expected things would turn out bad like this. Who is that man? Who is Dorian?'

'I don't know,' said Florentino. 'Nobody does. He was someone who came into my life full of promises and turned out to be evil. You know as much about him as I do, Mario. I tried to get close, but he would never let me get near to him.'

Nadja laughed, but it was the bitter quasi-hysterical laughter of an incomplete woman. Florentino observed the jerky, out-of-balance contradictions in his masculine and feminine polarities, the whole disordered mechanism that comprised Nadja's sexuality. But when the latter focused, it was with a concentrated singularity that had Florentino catch his breath and avert his eyes.

'I know more about Dorian than anyone,' he said, with a diva's husky genderless tone. Nadja poured himself another glass of wine and looked directly at Florentino.

'Keep away from that man. If you loved him, forget it. I could tell you things about Dorian Gray which would make you leave Venice tonight. Dorian Gray? I doubt you know anything of his past. I am rich with what you lack.'

Florentino felt the constriction tighten in his throat. He was pinned, and there was nowhere to go. He was being faced with the deconstruction of his past and the apparent dissolution of his future. He wanted neither to help nor to betray the man whom he had loved. In his mind, Dorian's hair was slipping through the wind again on their first meeting, and he was pushing his sunglasses upwards from his eyes. He saw him sipping his stone-cold glass of champagne on the terrace while boats slipped by on the Grand Canal. And it was how he would remember summer for ever. Beauty, and a blue sky travelling towards infinity.

'The trouble with Dorian,' said Nadja, 'is that no one can ever find him. He is so slippery he travels through your fingers. There is no way of really finding him. He is here. He is there. He is nowhere. And if you do find out his address, even weirder things happen.'

'Such as?' asked Florentino.

'You'd laugh at me,' said Nadja with deadly seriousness, 'but the house moves. Or else I am going mad. I went along to his street today and searched up and down it for an hour, and I couldn't find the place.'

'What do you want with him?' inquired Florentino, psychologically enlisting Mario's support and finding himself just the tiniest bit defensive of his former lover.

'I could say it is something karmic,' said Nadja. 'He and I

were drawn together for a purpose. I also stand for a community that I do not wish to see destroyed by this man. You are lucky to have got out alive. Others have disappeared.'

Florentino caught his breath. It was as though an ice-pack had been placed at the base of his spine. The chill telescoped up into his brain.

'He's too spooky for me,' said Mario. 'I have always been drawn to weird things, but Dorian is too much. I am thinking of going away for a while. I don't want him round looking for me.'

'Are you really so scared?' asked Florentino, looking across the line in which Mario's thick black curls fluffed out over a white collar. In his immediate perception of Mario, he felt sorry for his friend's difference. He could do nothing about his feminine eyes and the natural pout that was one of his female characteristics. His thin shoulders and tight waist further emphasised his androgyny.

'I'm terrified,' Mario said. 'I wish now I had never become involved. I wake up in the night and I imagine he is watching me.'

Florentino threw a studied look at the flagstones. The light was there, the same light arrived from a dead star, picking out an atomistic pattern on a particular stone lipped with dry moss. In the details on which he focused he recognised the impossibility of ever connecting with the phenomenal world. So much of his life had been absorbed by inanimate components. All the streets he had walked down, the places he had observed and known, they were so separate from his needs, and yet were a part of him. He could remember every summer of his life, and the ones that had happened a long time ago seemed as close to him as his feet were to the ground. He realised there could never be any distance between his past and the present. He was situated in himself, and that circumference was boundless. It touched upon everything everywhere.

Nadja held his glass up to the light. The wine in it blushed in the direct sunbeam. Nadja studied each fine detail of his gestures, self-consciously adjusting both his nervous input and its correlating external gesture. He appeared to Florentino to be contemplating a profound metaphysical dilemma, and he had an intimation that it was murder which preoccupied Nadja's mind. He could feel him turning the weapon over and over in his head, debating on the impacted force necessary not only to kill Dorian, but to appease the anger he felt every day of his life for ever, hour after hour, day after day.

Nadja sat for some time holding his self-dramatised pose, as though he was a model in a life-drawing class. His demeanour of self-qualified contempt combined with arrogant self-appraisal made him seem in Florentino's eyes as unapproachable as Dorian. Florentino knew he was troubled, for his mind kept on backtracking to childhood. He found himself taking refuge in sunny spaces, uncomplicated enclaves in which his mother was chopping onions on a bare wooden table and his father was back from the sea, maladjusted, sex-starved and unsociable. He would lift him on to his knees with his big hands and talk of adventure, islands, the tropical sun, and Florentino's favourite subject, smugglers. His head was exploding with the past. The isolated vignettes fizzed.

Nadja brought his glass down to his lap. His thoughts came down too, and it was as though he was picking up a tangible splinter from his head as he said with impacted venom, 'I don't want Dorian to be numbered amongst the living, but his death has to be the right one.'

Florentino experienced the chilling realisation that he was unwillingly being coerced into the role of accomplice. So much of what was happening was going on independent of him, as if he had lost all control over his life and was the spectator to an involuntary film screened outside him. He would have liked to get up and walk away, disowning any involvement in the whole ramified affair surrounding Dorian and his cult.

'No one is to speak of these things, I take it you all understand that,' Nadja was saying. 'I don't want to have to argue my point. We are all involved in this, and I don't want leakage to the police. Tell me what hours Dorian keeps, Florentino. And don't lie.'

Florentino was shocked into the awareness that Nadja was addressing him with quiet but authoritative severity. Nadja was implicating him directly by referring to a personal knowledge that he alone had of Dorian's movements. Nadja appeared to make it easier for him by saying, 'He's nocturnal, isn't he? Or at least he always was in Paris.'

'He is a night person,' Florentino fumbled. 'At least in my experience,' he added, partly swallowing his words and resenting the embarrassment that rushed to his cheeks. There was no way of not answering Nadja. His eyes and his voice asserted a transparent control over his listener. But already racing across Florentino's mind was the awareness that Dorian also had a place in the day, and would often slip out to the streets in one of his interminable disguises. The sunglassed Dorian protected by inscrutable black wrap-arounds from all inquisitive eyes.

'You are thinking about it, I hope,' said Nadja, as though reading the impulses on a polygraph.

'Well, sometimes he goes out in the day – I don't know. What is it you want of me?' Florentino again felt a sense of betraying Dorian. A pressure was working him from the inside to confess. And despite the heat, there was a cold rivulet of sweat travelling down his spine.

'You don't know the half of it,' he said with unnatural rapidity, causing Nadja to swing his averted head round in a semicircle and to sneer contemptuously.

'I know more about Dorian Gray than he does about himself,' Nadja responded, turning on Florentino, his voice cuttingly controlled and kept in a quiet register. Florentino and Mario were visibly diminished by the malevolent concentration of Nadja's voice. Nadja could have cut cloth with his vocal cords.

'There are big holes in your thinking,' Nadja directed at both Florentino and Mario. 'You seem unaware of Dorian's true character. In Paris, he was called the devil. It was rumoured he was so terrible that not even the police would touch him. People fear any sort of contact with him. His interests are not in sex, they are in the devil. He'll burn all of you.'

Nadja emptied his glass and Mario obediently refilled it. Nadja's ability to inject compulsive subservience in others was pronounced by his understated authority. The energy in him quivered like a whip awaiting the hand of a dominatrix. He was like a cobra vibrating to trigger a kill.

'The devil,' Nadja re-emphasised. 'This man's got inside all of us. He is black. He has broken out on my skin in the form of nervous rashes. He is even there in my sleep. It is my role to track him down. They have rat-catchers in Paris. I'm a Dorian catcher.'

Florentino was torn again between his own total denunciation of Dorian, and feelings of residual compassion for the man Nadja evidently intended to murder. He looked at Nadja's startlingly improvised features. He seemed like Dorian's counterpart in perversity. He could see how each would prove an intolerable reminder to the other of all that was insufferable about the shadow. Each expressed what was unredemptive in the other. Florentino wanted to confess everything, he felt the need to release a whole stream of troubled images and memories, but he bit on his pain and held it back. However, each time the pressure travelled back to his diaphragm and rose towards his throat. He had only to speak and a torrent would rush out. He was choking on the uroborous of past and present, degradation and grief.

Nadja's eyes found him again. They danced over his pain. Florentino had the biting apprehension that Nadja knew everything which was inside him. Every word. He would count them as they were spoken. Thirty, three hundred, three thousand, thirty thousand. Could you really measure pain by words?

'Why don't you come out with it,' Nadja said, as though he wasn't really speaking at all but just helping Florentino to clear his conscience. 'You know something and I know something and together it will add up. I have all day to hear you out – and remember, cutie, I am on your side.'

Mario had totally withdrawn from the conversation. He sat shrunk into himself, distracted, the worry showing in his blank eyes. He was trying to pretend he was not there. He had grown to be the immobilised sculpture of himself, hands resting on his raised knees, his chin balanced on his arms. It looked for the moment that if he could stop his thoughts, then he might also be able to stop time. The whole group would form a frozen tableau extracted from continuous momentum.

'All right,' Florentino abruptly volunteered, 'I'll tell you what I can.'

There was a silence in which Florentino telescoped into the

chaos of his inner life. The past was a series of disconnected visual fragments, sense-associations, deintensified transmissions. Some of it had been assembled into words, and Florentino found a pivot in what was uppermost in his throat.

'He has destroyed me,' he seethed, more in the way of a spasm than as measured articulation. 'He has twisted everything in which I have ever believed. He has taken away the simple things by which I once lived. I have met evil. I have met what you call the devil. And I have lost everything. My family. The place in which I lived. The lot.'

'More importantly,' Nadja cut in, 'you lost yourself. And that is the greatest loss of all.'

'I believed in him,' Florentino rejoined. 'He promised me everything and then went dead on me. He has sucked out my blood.'

Nadja evinced no trace of compassion for Florentino. He appeared to be looking at an invisible spot on the wall that he could reach only by staring straight through Florentino to the other side. His natural resting-point with his eyes was one of unnervingly detached scrutiny.

'But whatever happens, I won't be a party to killing him,' Florentino added. 'You do what you like, but leave me out of it. I am not interested in violence.'

'No one has spoken of violence,' said Nadja, in an undertow of subtle implications. 'That's not my scene. Besides, this meeting never took place, as I have told you. Get that in your heads.'

Florentino felt a taste of rust in his throat. He was swallowing on tarnished saliva. He could feel his life travelling down a bottomless slide to nowhere. Whatever stood up in the abdominal pit was hugely reproachful. It was Dorian's redoubtable chimera threatening retribution which knocked violently in his heart.

'He no longer goes to San Michele,' Florentino volunteered. 'He has been frightened off. The cult has disbanded. This means he stays at home more, sometimes for days on end, and also goes out during the day. He employs no one now. He doesn't trust anyone. There is a side-entrance to the house which goes into an alley. Dorian uses it to come and go. A dark-blue door.'

The inquisitive tension in Nadja's face dispersed. He let go his hostility and smiled, and then, as if to conceal his pleasure, returned to a measure of severity. His thin body gave him the appearance of a whip resting vertically in a chair. His eyes checked his two cowed victims for any trace of shared complicity. He manipulated Florentino and Mario on a dual energy beam. They were passive automatons he had programmed for information. They would talk and shut up at his command. He felt close to having extracted what would initially be of use to him. There were pips left in the orange, but these could be sucked out at another time.

'And do you know anything additional?' Nadja shot at Mario, who jerked back to himself and immediately said 'No'.

'I am taking you both on trust,' said Nadja. 'Don't let me be disappointed. I know where I can find you, so I will be back.'

The vibrant hammering was taken up again in the next-door shipping-yard, the heavy unresilient sound of metal hitting metal echoing with percussive menace. Nadja flinched from the intrusive overload. He treated the intrusion like an affrontive slap in the face. It was the signal for him to get up and leave, his ostentatious figure seeming to dematerialise in the light, as he let himself out into the street.

Florentino did not move. He heard the door to the street shut and breathed in deeply, grateful for the space that flooded back with its reassuring personal ambience. Mario too unfolded from his rigid posture and stared at Florentino with evident disbelief that it had all ever happened. The sunlight was still the same light transmitted from the same star, and the immediate city noises had altered in their backdrop regulation. The shipbuilders in the yard next door had no conceivable idea of events that had occurred on the other side of the wall. Florentino was made aware of the separateness of events, and the existential alienation of all things from others. He could feel the blood humming in his veins, and there was this big blue spatial curve overhead which was the sky. He could not make the connection between the two, but he felt it existed somewhere in the universe.

Mario poured the last of the wine and held it out to Florentino like a symbolic bruise delivered by Nadja's threat. They sat in the warmth of the closed yard, each too apprehensive to speak. The sunlight swelled like the warm fur of a cat.

Mario bunched his hands in his pockets. The lack of developed masculinity in him prevented him from channelling his wounded emotions into male hostility. Florentino could see that the boy wanted to go. His nervousness, his manifest wish to disengage from any future associations with Dorian or Nadja were evident in the resigned expression in his eyes. He placed his hand in Florentino's, looked into his eyes and was gone without a word. Florentino heard the gate close for a second time and the hurried sound of Mario's feet tripping away through the alley. He went over and secured the bolt and returned to his seat under the fig tree. A deep cobalt shadow had swung into his place, its cool imprint mapping out an opaque bar on the flagstones. Florentino felt totally alone. He was an exile in his native city, a fugitive hiding from friends and enemies alike. He tasted his own sense of ravaged awkwardness. He was not a part of any recognisable social order. He had no job and no place of his own. He was someone who lived on edges, and he had ended up badly cutting his feet. He would quickly run out of the little money he had stolen from Dorian, and then he would have to steal or make a liaison with a tourist in order to survive. Neither was a world to which he wished to return. He ruminated on the possibilities open to him in life. They seemed so few in proportion to the size and diversity of the universe. His existence had contracted to the microdot of a yard. His options were destructively ruinous.

Florentino sat for a long time with his head in his hands. The shipyard was quiet now, the workers must have gone home, and the quarter was silent. The yard was broody and impregnated with history. Florentino wondered if his feet were not stood flat on sunken blood. He was fidgety and wanted to go out, but fear restrained him. The eye would be watching. Dorian's or Nadja's. The big eye that would burn through the back of his head. The omniscient eye that missed nothing and tracked everything. And he feared internally that Dorian knew his actions without having to witness their external manifestation. Florentino froze into a sense of unmitigated isolation. He was isolated outside time. He had been extracted from the rhythm that had run through his days, no matter how tenuous, and now felt dislodged from all purpose in his life. He had nothing to do but reflect on the circumstances that had resulted in his being a fugitive. He felt victimised and unable to own to any culpability for his actions. His life with Dorian had appeared unreal, and as a consequence he felt unable fully to identify with the past. It could have been anyone's past but it was his. He found that difficult to swallow. He would have liked to disown every action that failed to conform with his idea of himself. He thought of going home and asking his mother for shelter, but that would have been a humiliating concession to defeat. It would have been an admission of failure which he felt unable to countenance. His mother would have looked up from her chair and realised that something was wrong. She would have scented his inner distress, and skirted the issue, preparing to tolerate all irregularities because he was her son, but none the less knowing it was a bad reason that brought him back home. He thought he would rather go on the streets than succumb to that humiliation. He had outgrown every reason that would have him return to his mother except the idea of maternal protection. The notion of hunger had never occurred to him before, and he tried to accommodate his mind to the distinct possibility that he would lack food. He had a loaf of bread indoors and a bottle of wine, but nothing more. The friend who was letting him use the place was off with a lover for a week, and so his acute awareness of isolation deepened. He didn't know what to do with himself. Had he not suspected he was under surveillance he would have gone to a bar, or he would have been in conversation with a middle-aged American tourist in a hotel lobby. He could conjure the fragrant scent of cigar smoke filtered from the stranger's mouth, the repressed lubricity living in his eyes as a series of desperately understated appeals for recognition. A man. He had known so many. They were all in this city to find what they could not tolerate in themselves. Florentino was a part of that game. He had enjoyed the adulation of being desired from an early age. Men came on at him before he had even decided if he was interested in his own sex. And so the process of being treated as a woman by other men had exclusively narrowed his perceptions. He had no need to desire women, for he was treated as one by men. Looking back over his life he could see that it had begun early, and without his being aware of the anomaly. Eyes in the crowd had baptised him with his difference. He could remember in a series of flashbacks waiting for his mother outside a shop, and a grey-suited stranger, heady with a woody tang of cologne, just standing there smiling at him with such a complicitous look of induction into a shared secret that he had turned away distressed and run into the pharmacy to claim his mother, who knew nothing of the encounter. He had always refused to enter the pharmacist's because of the obsessive attention the owner gave to his mother. The man used to give his mother stockings, and on that particular afternoon Florentino was rewarded with barley sugar for having overcome his dislike of the shop. His mother had bought him a green comb, and although he resolutely avoided the pharmacist's eyes, his presence in the shop seemed to bring the man closer to his mother. It all came back to him as he sat dejected in the increasing shade. He knew now that the pharmacist was having an affair with his mother while his father was away at sea. At the time he had experienced resentment that anyone should distract his mother from his constant need for attention, and he recalled the time he had come home from school too early, instinct telling him that his mother's throaty orgasmic shrieks were pleasure rather than pain. He had stood at the foot of the stairs for a long time and heard the violent commotion from the squeaky bed upstairs, fear and excitement alternating in him as the rhythm overhead reached a cataclysmic crescendo before the house subsided into its customary silence.

Animated flashbacks lit up his mind with random footage. Things leapt out of one year into another with no sequential connection. He ran through summers building up to the one in which he had met Dorian. Long white days on the Lido, the hot dazzle of sand under his bare feet. He would take a towel there every day and sit looking out at the ultramarine reach of the lagoon. Someone would always come up and join him. And there would be drinks later on terraces overlooking the sea. Couples would flirt outrageously on the promenade. There were girls in bikinis who looked back at him but he never took up with their advances. All those summer people streaming through. Where did they all go to, he wondered? Summers were the same all over the world. A time for romantic and sexual liberties, a time in which to perpetuate the illusion that youth lasted for ever. Everyone seemed to walk direct down a corridor and disappear into the sea.

He jolted in and out of a recapitulative retrogression. In one vision a girl was being passionately made love to under the sea wall, just as the darkness dropped, and in another his mother was sitting on the edge of her bed, rolling on the silk film of first one stocking and then the other. She was drawing the tops taut against black suspender-straps. The stockings were of course a gift from the pharmacist. He jumped from one phased vignette to the next. All the cameras, sunglasses, martinis and boat excursions across the lagoon which comprised marine summers. All the little details of people and places flooded back, as though they were sites implanted in his mind. Pistachio ices and Ambre Solaire and the kelp smell of the sea riffled his olfactory memory. And then that one day, that special day when he had encountered Dorian for the first time, showed up blindingly huge on the image-film.

He got up from where he was sitting, went indoors, and fetched the remaining bottle of wine. The pulled cork was the colour of a girl's lipstick at the tip. He drank two glasses in quick succession and warmed to the comforting afterglow. The wine put an enlivened flush to his cornered situation. It occurred to him that he could act to remedy his position rather than accept the passive role consigned to a victim. His thinking had contracted to the grid in which he was imprisoned. There was a way out somewhere and he had to find it. As he sat there, a rat ran abruptly across the yard and into hiding. The creature had grown genetically programmed by fear to consider itself always a fugitive. He had no wish to extend the analogue to his own underworld species. He would break out of the trap and live. He finished a third glass of wine and resolved to act from temerity. He shut the house door, put on a light jacket, strode confidently across the yard and let himself out. It was twilight and the sky was a stormy violet. He walked down the alley connecting with the street, his paranoia anticipating immediate arrest by a rough hand on his shoulder, or the singular bark of a pistol calculated to put a bullet in his spine. He swung his head over his shoulder, hallucinating Nadja's slim figure standing watching him, but there was no one there. He could smell a mephitic tang from the canals. The water was toxic with chemical effluvia. He had heard it said that the plague moved over its surface as a black hand, and that that hand singled out individuals in the crowd and marked them. A pat on the back would mean a slow, convulsive death.

Florentino hurried on. He was not sure of his direction, but he knew he would end up in Dorian's street. Lights were coming on in the alleys. Little yellow planets that would burn all night, sheltering the human from the vastness of the abstract dark. Fractals of light geometricised the absolutely still water. When a breeze ran across the surface it was like a guitar string being tuned. The water slackened again, clearing itself of chaos. Florentino hurried on, almost tripping over a hawser. A gondola came down the canal at an even measure, a red lantern illuminating its prow. It looked like a coffin being rowed through the underworld. Its wake dissolved like oil on the bottle-green water.

Florentino could feel the gravitational pull in his footsteps towards Dorian's street. With no conscious effort on his part he was being directed home. It was a sort of magnetism, a compulsion to return to the scene of his ruin. He was already picking up on his homecoming. There was nowhere else to go. He either retraced his steps or followed to the end. Even the scent of the streets was growing familiar, as a cocktail of urinous and cooking smells which hung out in corners and characterised the neighbourhood. There was the local café three streets away from Dorian's, its interior lit by red lamps, the tobacconist's, the stationer's, the unkempt black labrador lying at the entrance to a yard; there was the sound of excited voices issuing from a top-floor apartment; and over all the fired-up state of his nerves. All of his senses were on dangerous overkill. He kept remembering the story of a woman who had committed suicide at the Lido, leaving her red coat on the white sands as a dramatic valediction to the world before she walked out naked into the winter sea. The image of her abandoned red coat kept on arresting his progress. There was something in this symbol that held a direct association with the painful experiences he had known with Dorian. And he knew deep within himself that he should keep away. To return seemed an invitation to ruin. He was going back because he felt unsuited to cope with life outside of sheltered parameters. He was too disaffiliated from his background to look for employment compatible with his education and temperament. Rising within him too was a brutal masochistic awareness of self-destruction. He knew that Dorian faced imminent catastrophe and he was attracted to the idea of dying with him, or of being sacrificed for his cause. Dorian's immersion in the occult, and the sado-sexual characteristics that had given Florentino no recourse but to get out of the house and out of his life, were now the repellent attraction to which he found himself returning.

All the while he was expecting to encounter Nadja waiting in alleys, at street corners, as the androgynised personification of revenge. Nadja appeared like a platinum-haired spook left over from the carnival. Florentino sensed that he was being watched, but he no longer cared. He wanted to get back and make his peace with Dorian, who would probably be drugged and incoherent. He had grown used to the aesthetic accoutrements that were a part of their life together. He tried to delude himself with the notion that he would go back, steal money from Dorian, and then break with him definitively. Scheme after scheme jolted up on display in his mind. And nagging at him concurrently was the fear that perhaps Dorian had changed the locks or gone away. What if he could not get into the apartment? He consoled himself with the idea that he would break in if necessary and steal whatever valuables he could convert into money. Rings, perfumes, bracelets, scarves, all would be easy to sell to his milieu. Dorian kept a fortune in jewellery concealed in his bedroom and private study. He would fist out clusters of emeralds and sapphires and make a break for it. He knew that Dorian was a wanted man and would never contact the police about theft. But then he knew Dorian would destroy him through occult machinations. He would blow the fuses on his nerves.

He saw himself paralysed, the flames jumping out of his body in a scene of explosive autocombustion.

The street was empty. There were house lights on in the alley, and Florentino anticipated Nadja jumping out at him from a doorway. Or he imagined Nadja waiting for him in Dorian's sumptuous apartment, his diffident all-the-time-in-the-world manner presiding over the drawing-room as he waited for Dorian to return home.

He stood on the corner for a long time, debating whether to go forward or to stay. Cooking smells brushed his nostrils. He badly wanted shelter, even if that meant the continuation of some sort of life with Dorian. He felt over-exposed to a world he considered hostile. He would always be an outsider, a social outlaw living on the fringes of society. In his mind he knew that if he survived Dorian he would move on to another rich stranger. He had grown accustomed to a life-style in which the young pasha was supported by a nominal husband. It was the fear of poverty that sent him back up the narrow alley like someone walking up a gun-barrel. He could feel himself shaking inside. He had lost his immediate fear of Nadja in the loaded apprehension of re-encountering Dorian. He fingered the keys in his jeans pocket. He knew the keys would admit him to life or death. In his hallucinated way he staged the possibility of Dorian's suicide. He imagined the latter lying on the floor surrounded by a huge circle of red roses, the gun blown out of his hand to the floor, a rusty trickle of congealed blood escaping from his lipsticked mouth. He fantasised that he would discover him slumped over his altar, his face twisted from the scouring toxicity of poison. He imagined Dorian bloated and spotted like a green fungus. His heart was racing with tachycardiac rapidity. It sounded like a drum-machine inside a hollow cave.

He took out his back-door key, the serrations comfortably finding their grooves in the lock. Relief flooded through his body. It had always surprised Florentino that Dorian lived with minimal house security, but he realised now it was because of his self-protective occult powers. No one would dare break through that impregnable ambience. Once inside the back door, he stood at the bottom of a flight of stone steps that would take him to a passage which connected with the main living area. He listened. There was no sound at all, but already his nostrils were picking up on strains of the subtle incense that pervaded Dorian's rooms, a Japanese scent that seemed incessantly to recycle itself as a permanently invasive subtext to Dorian's life. It was there, part reassuring, part nauseous to his raw, jumpy nerves.

Florentino stood in the dark passage. There was a lateral splinter of light showing under the connecting door. He could sense Dorian's presence somewhere in that interior, like a silk-shirted minotaur brooding centre stage to the labyrinth. His heart still sounded as though someone was shaking a stone inside a cardboard box.

He opened the connecting door with his second key, wondering if he would be blown apart by psychic explosive as he entered, but there was no uptake on the other side. There was just the impacted silence that always surrounded Dorian. A rich mosaic of Persian rugs carpeted Florentino's footsteps, the whorled grotto of blues and reds giving the floor an underwater feel, as though it was a tropical sea-bed being observed through a glass panel in a boat. An ebony sphinx presided over the room, its ambiguous feline characteristics investing the place with mystic undertones. Florentino moved towards their communal drawing-room, where Dorian would sometimes sit distractedly at the Steinway, feeling for a music that always eluded him. Florentino's eyes jumped to the familiar red velvet armchairs, but Dorian was not there, sitting in a drugged stupor, as so often was his way. The drinks table was loaded with a slewed clutter of bottles, some of them left unstoppered, and Dorian had clearly poured out four or five different mixes of spirits so that he could move from glass to glass in accordance with the needs of his palate. Florentino snatched at a tumbler of whisky and gulped hard. A trail of mellow fire opened up in the pit of his stomach. He assessed that Dorian would be in his bedroom, either ritualistically dressing for the coming night or slumped on the bed from excesses. Both states were familiar to Florentino, and so was the sweet after-scent of the joint Dorian must have smoked earlier. The room was not only a compendium of his decadent tastes but a register of his habits.

Florentino made his way quietly towards the bedroom. The door was ajar, and Florentino could feel Dorian's body space on the inside. A broody abstract opacity, simmering with contradictory expressions of the perverse. He put his hand round the door as a sign to Dorian that he was home and then insinuated himself into the bedroom, with its heavy purple drapes and purple velvet curtains. Dorian was sitting in a chair staring right at him without saying a word. His catatonic eyes were the measure of whatever substance he was using. Their compulsively singular power freaked Florentino into an exclamation of fear and surprise. Dorian was dressed in a red silk shirt, and there was a glass bowl full of cocaine crystals beside him. He was clearly coming down from a high, and he looked wasted from lack of food yet still imperiously formidable in the concentration of his energies. He was coked and interiorised. He stared out of a madhouse of delusional fantasies. Florentino was left totally on the outside of a psychotic screen. Dorian ignored him, lined up some more cocaine, snorted, and then reconnected with reality. Florentino doubted that he knew he had ever been away, but the cold reserve in Dorian's eyes told him that his betrayal had been recorded with punitive hostility. He wanted to go up to Dorian and hold him, but he froze in the act, terrified of overt rejection. All of Dorian's childish egocentricity, the self-indulgent monocentric universe he inhabited was visible in his air of injurious sleight. 'You'll pay for this,' he snarled at Florentino. 'No one betrays me and lives. You should know it's the condition of our pact. Where have you been?'

'I needed to go away and think,' said Florentino, nervous that his subterfugal inner schemes were visible to Dorian's alarmingly transparent scrutiny. 'I got scared, but look, I'm back again and I'm not going to go away.'

Dorian stared at him as if he were abject flotsam, a thin smile cutting like a wire across his sealed lips. His emaciated body and the girlish slimness of his hips afforded him a disconcertingly boyish appearance even in his state of drugged ravage. His hair was the colour of sunlight. In his red silk shirt he could have been mistaken for a youth of twenty-one. He continued to stare at Florentino as though unstitching his mind seam by seam in a form of laser surgery.

'You'll pay when we return to San Michele,' Dorian admonished. 'You'll be the final sacrifice. You will join the castrati and become a transsexual.' He laughed. 'A man with a woman's body. Done on the altar.'

Florentino retracted into himself. He wanted to run out of the house, but he checked himself, conscious he would wait his time and risk stealing valuable pieces of jewellery. He could no longer find the compassion within him to meet Dorian's drug habit with sympathetic allowance. Too many bad events had come to block his emotions. He realised, standing there, watching Dorian's pathologically dangerous condition, that he had never been qualified to share this man's life. He had mistaken power for glamour. He had been attracted to the surface reflection of a poisonous lake. He could no longer love a man who had become so estranged from reality. He no longer knew who Dorian was and doubted that he had ever penetrated his inscrutably defensive inner world. The man was not human, but his engagingly youthful and romantic looks continued to assert a compelling fascination.

Florentino was still unable to let that go. Dorian's blue eyes always stopped his breath. And he watched the play of rings on fingers so perfectly elongated that they seemed to be feeling for some invisible frequency. Florentino's heart was being torn open in the arena. He wanted to shout out to Dorian that he hated him. He wanted to curse him for ever entering his life, but he could not do so. He wanted to shout out that he loved him as well as despised him, but again he could not. The words were not there. There was just the big freeze.

'Harry called today,' Dorian said with alarming clarity. 'You have never met him. He ran out on me too. Lord Henry Wotton. Harry to me. He risked his repaired marriage and renewed social status in coming here. He wanted to warn me my life is in danger.'

Dorian laughed again, a contemptuous, parched laugh, part presided over by the belief in his indestructibility and part bitter at the acute sense of isolation that had come to invest his life with a feeling of terminal abandonment. Florentino had noticed how even the succession of houseboys had stopped coming. The apartment was dehumanised. It was like a cage housing a progenitor of abnormality.

'Harry hasn't really changed,' Dorian said, as if to himself. 'People never do. They simply answer the needs of their immediate situation. But he came disguised. It was only the voice I recognised at first. Said his wife thought he was away on business affairs in Zurich, and he had been, but he felt compelled to come here. He was trying to redeem himself for having betrayed me. He has spoken about me too often and too explicitly to a network. Everything filters through, if you know what I mean. Word about me hangs in the air like bacteria on these canals.

'But Harry, his past is as dark as mine. I shouldn't tell you these things, but my audience is reduced. I am in retreat from everyone,' Dorian reflected. 'Harry was the one love of my life, and if events had not been complicated, we would still be together. But we went down. I can't tell you much. But Harry disappeared from my life. I have shared a lot of my past with him. Too much. It is as if I have given him a huge transfusion of myself. More of my blood than I have left for myself, and still I do not know if I love him or hate him for what he has done to me. He has put a name and a price on me, but I am not afraid.'

Florentino stood back and observed Dorian's impenetrable demeanour. There was no way through his defences. He was resolutely withdrawn into a cocaine-halo, and into a world over which he autocratically presided. He was playing a film back in his head. Harry must have been speeding through his mind in a series of animated clips.

'I have rituals to perform in the coming weeks,' Dorian resumed. 'You will stay here at the apartment with me, and we shall go back to San Michele and enact the final one.'

'What do you mean,' Florentino asked, 'by the final ritual?' He felt an instant fear at the enormity of Dorian's threat. He assumed from Dorian's earlier speech that he was alluding again to human sacrifice. The conviction reasserted itself in Florentino's mind that Dorian was mad. He was using magic as his sole expression of reality. His composure was that of one of the indestructibles. Florentino felt a revival of compassion in him for Dorian's ruined condition. He felt he could not abandon the man he had loved to total isolation. And even though he had heard so much said about Dorian's nefarious criminality and the murders attributed to him, part of him would not believe any of it. He knew in his heart he would stay, even though he should have acted to the contrary.

Dorian got up from his chair and went over and propped himself up on the bed. His leopard-skin shoes rested on the mauve silk counterpane. His hair poured on a quincunx of cushions. There was a hookah placed next to the bed, and an arrangement of books on the bedside table. He lay back in a recapitulative mood.

'I'm in the light,' he said. 'I'll blast anyone who comes near me. This is an offensive and not a retreat. I am not in hiding from the world as a fugitive, I am preparing the few for a new order. You will see. The miraculous will occur. Harry will be back to follow the chosen. Harry is with his wife again. I took him from a woman and he has gone back to one. Harry used to buy me shirts to match the colours of the sunset. And if you want to know, it was he who encouraged me in the road I have taken. It was Harry who brought out the capacity for magic in me. I have become the fulfilment of what for him remains purely potential. He is frightened of me, for he has seen me live out his own unrealised destiny. And for that reason his love is split into hate. You will understand these things later on in life. Some kinds of love feed and destroy at the same time, and neither expression becomes separated from the other. That is the most twisted sort of love, but it can be the most sexually stimulating. But I would not have Harry return for anything. That is all in the past. Harry is sold into death.'

Florentino let Dorian free-associate with his stream of inner dialogue. The past and the present took their collisional course. Dorian stared into the interior of his unconscious. The night outside was silent. The house could have been under water, a construct swallowed by the creeping waters of the lagoon, coloured fish nosing against the house walls. He imagined the foundations walking out to sea, a somnambulist building browsing through the coral- and weed-encrusted hulls of wrecks. Florentino watched Dorian flake out. He left him lying on the bed, went into the other room and sat at the piano. He had never played one in his life, but he attacked the keys with ferocity, fisting the ivories and giving violent expression to his rage. He thumped his emotions out, and then went and ate with primal avidity. He wanted to sleep and wake up to a new day. One in which the world and Dorian would have been completely transformed.

 *Chapter 8*

DORIAN tentatively opened the curtains to take note of the day. A translucent turquoise sky, a colour familiar to the city in October, curved above St Mark's. He was not sure what time it was, but he could hear the city's buzz of commerce, and closer by the sound of Florentino performing inexpert finger exercises at the piano. The city was a system of interactive communications from which he was excluded. He was unnervingly aware of his isolation and the way his life functioned through a parallel dimension. He drew the curtains and felt the cutting-edge of his solitude. He was intensely aware that Nadja was watching him somewhere, but he was sure of his own safety. He was convinced that even if Nadja emptied a gun through his heart, he would walk away unhurt.

Dorian felt estranged from himself, his dissociative mood was asking to be addressed. He was uncomfortable and disquieted, and he wondered if he was being spooked by the residue of a dream, the chimerical afterglow of some oneiric trauma. He could not recollect anything from his night dreams, or the circumstances surrounding his falling asleep. He knew he would have been drugged and that at some stage he would have lapsed into unconsciousness and that Florentino would have come into the room and put him beneath the silk counterpane. His nights were a compendium of various substances punctuated by alcohol. For Dorian this interposed a screen between himself and the past. Forgetting was a way of disengaging from chronology. It placed him outside linearity and the causal connections to time. He had reinvented himself through the study of magic, but there was something wrong inside today. He was out of tune with his rhythms and at odds with himself. He could smell a premonition of catastrophe, and sensed that he was about to confront terror. He stalked uneasily about the room, avoiding mirrors, tense, as though he was contained by walls at every movement. The image of a tiger throwing itself against bars jumped into his head. He fumbled himself a first glass of whisky, adding water to assuage his conscience over the unnaturally early hour of his having a first drink. Or was it afternoon? He was not sure, but familiarity with the volume of noise transmitted by the outside world told him it was morning.

He went over to the mirror and was blown back by what he observed. His once golden hair was liberally streaked with grey, and his face had aged in the course of the night. His skin was sagging and a network of lines were to be seen under his eyes and in the hollow of his cheeks. The tight, youthful profile of his high cheekbones had dramatically lost effect and tension. Dorian was horrified by what he saw. He believed that a gradual reversal in the portrait's condition must be taking place. It appeared impossible to him that Basil Hallward's portrait may have been returning to the artist's original intention of portraying immutable youth, and that his own body would now revert to natural ageing. The reversal had appeared impossible, as long as he had maintained optimum control over his life as a practitioner of the occult. But his dissipation, he suspected, had left him vulnerable to upsetting the original pact he had made with the painting to have it express immutable youth.

Dorian knew he had to take immediate action, for he had no intention of allowing Florentino to see him old or ravaged. He hurried into the black marble bathroom adjoining his bedroom. The careful application of foundation, and the introduction of dye to his hair would save appearances. But now the process had begun, he feared its rapid acceleration. He would be fighting a war against cellular decay, and it was something he could not face. Dorian had always kept a large stock of make-up in his bathroom, and he applied moisturiser and foundation to repair the damage, although something about his unchangeable youth had gone. He locked the door to prevent Florentino's inadvertently entering, and over the course of the next hour bleached his hair, obsessively searching to annihilate every vestige of grey roots. Dorian was happy with the restoration of his hair colour, but he remained deeply unnerved by the overall alteration in his features. He could not believe that he had looked like this yesterday. Paranoia raced through his mind that he had aged before Florentino had left his room last night. Or had he been walking around like this for weeks in his disorientated condition?

Having temporarily restored his looks, he put on a mauve satin shirt and called Florentino to his room. The boy came in with no trace of suspicion in his eyes. Dorian felt over-exposed and was constantly in danger of losing his nerve. He could not afford to risk the redoubtable control he exerted over Florentino. In his own eyes he was projecting the image of himself as old and broken. He saw himself on the opposite wall, valetudinarian, impoverished, an object of ridicule by youth. His antipathetic shadow mobbed his consciousness. He resented the antinomy with a white-hot suppressed rage. Florentino reassured him that it was mid-morning and that there had been no callers. Dorian's mind went back to his London days and the times when Harry had called, often without advance warning, and of the ominous day on which he had brought with him the news of Sibyl Vane's suicide. That was another life. London was buried in his unconscious like a city swallowed by the ocean. Harry was somewhere and nowhere and everywhere, a figure who would find resolution with neither sex. And yet he had left an arrow in Dorian's heart. It smoked and bled in fifty shades of vermilion.

Florentino asked Dorian if he wanted his Turkish coffee for breakfast, and the dish of fruit soaked in cognac at which he would pick with a spoon. After his capricious breakfast, Florentino would bring Dorian a glass of champagne and a cigar on a small silver tray, and so his day would begin. He would then listen to French songs on the expensive system in which he had invested, records by Charles Aznavour, Juliette Gréco and Serge

Lama. It was the same ritual each day. And Dorian sustained it out of habit no matter that his life was falling apart. He toyed with kiwi and strawberry segments soaked overnight in cognac and oddly for him requested that Florentino draw the curtains for half an hour. He put on dark glasses to continue with his breakfast, and let the mid-morning light wash through the room. Behind his dark-green lenses the sky appeared lilac. Florentino stood looking out of the window, elbows propped on the ledge, his eyes searching to left and right as though anticipating an intruder. Dorian had noticed the worried expression that had been written on his face for weeks. Florentino had come to look like someone being hunted out of his skin. And when Florentino drew back from the window opening on to the street he was drained of colour. 'He was out there last night,' he said to Dorian. 'We'd better be prepared.'

'Who are you talking about?' Dorian asked, attempting to simulate surprise at Florentino's nervous appraisal of the situation.

'Nadja. Who else could it be?' said Florentino. 'He was outside in the alley last night. I fear one of these days he will break in. Couldn't we go away? Leave by night and never return.'

'He would follow us to the end of the world,' Dorian replied. 'Nadja's as much inside me as he is outside. My only means of being free of him is to perform a ritual that will kill him. Don't worry. He would not dare come near me. He knows my power. He would be burnt the second he crossed the threshold.'

'We are not safe,' Florentino pleaded. 'Can't we leave tonight? You could have a cab collect us under cover of the dark.'

'We are staying,' said Dorian. 'It is Nadja who will disappear. I am going to work on him and then we shall be left alone. You know so little of my abilities.' Dorian left off speaking and paced around the room. He was tormented, and his strung-out nerves buzzed off the walls. He was like an animal trapped in a cage who was trying to divert attention from his predicament. He would swing round from his orbit and realise that there was nowhere to go.

Florentino was again torn between loyalty to his friend and the desire to disappear. He could run while the going was still good. He could listen to his feet clatter down the alley. He could head for the *vaporetto*, his pockets loaded with jewellery, and make a break to the mainland. But he was terrified of leaving his birthplace. Its narrow parameters had formed everything he had ever known of life. Its distribution of alleys and canals was written into his nerves. In his eyes, Dorian resembled a crazy tycoon, someone in a mauve satin shirt participating in his own ruin at a casino. He disappeared into the bedroom and Florentino knew he had gone to his cocaine-bowl. He used the stuff so liberally that he had complained of an eroded septum and nosebleeds. He had stopped eating proper meals, and now just idled with gourmet delicacies.

When Dorian came back into the room he said, 'Tonight we will celebrate my birthday. I have something in mind. I am not someone who remembers his age, but this time I wish to commemorate my birthday. Go out and buy extra candles.'

'I am afraid to go out,' Florentino said. 'Nadja and his friends may be watching the house.'

Dorian laughed. 'They won't harm you. You have my protection sealing you like an envelope. No one would dare come near you. But if you left me, if you ran away, they would shred you. They would come out of the alleys in a hunting pack.'

Florentino visualised Dorian's indirect threat. He saw himself in the middle of the day, in a city suddenly gone quiet, pursued from one complex to the next, a premonitory figure standing at the end of each alley he tried for escape. They would move in on him slowly, while he realised the terror of being manoeuvred into a cul-de-sac. A black shadow as big as a cloud and solid as an iron bar would eclipse his turning round. He had experienced nightmares in which this took place, the autonomous action beating him out of sleep to lie on the bed like a fish hauled into a boat and flailing for lack of oxygen.

Dorian wanted Florentino out of the house for a while. He was still unhappy with his appearance and needed to devote more time to checking a colour match for his hair, and to scrutinising his deteriorating features. Tonight he would take out the portrait and confront its state of irreparable defacement. Fear of reading the inner contents of his life in its malignant metamorphosis had kept him from examining the painting ever since he had been fascinated by its decay in London. At that time he had been compelled to consult the painting as a commentary on his shadow. And even though the canvas had been lacerated, he had sensed that the fissures had grown together again like skin. He ran his fingers over his cheeks, obsessed by their loss of taut contour. He was acutely sensitive to each cell in his tissue, and stared at his fingertips with their light dusting of porcelain foundation from contact with his face. He went straight to his large bedroom mirror, prepared himself, and then opened his eyes. He did not like what he saw, although his shining hair continued to give him an unnaturally youthful appearance. He considered how he had never known age, he had never acknowledged that his mind was in opposition to a failing organism. He had never caught sight of himself in a shop window and stood back at the apprehension of a stranger. He was outraged at this alteration to his fixed physical appearance. He wanted to smash the mirror to deny its truth. He consoled himself with the belief that he was seeing himself from the distorted perception induced by mind-bending drugs. But his fingers retracked evidence of lines in his face. There were small lateral hairlines and the beginnings of furrows in the cheeks. What Dorian had always dreaded was the irreversibility of age. He would have no control over its genetic mutations, and in the isolated moment of discovering it in himself he tasted for the first time an awareness of the limitations of mortality. Unable to believe fully in the image presented by one mirror, he consulted each mirror in the apartment, running from one to the other with a wild sense of incredulity impressed on his face. Right to the last mirror in Florentino's room he hoped for the return of his familiar features. He longed for his perennial youth to redress the arrival of pronounced middle age.

He found it hard to believe that Florentino had shown no gesture of surprise at the sudden change in his appearance. He kept on with the idea that his change was a subjective phenomenon which might not register externally. He thought perhaps he was ill and undergoing a breakdown, and that his nerves had finally exploded. He would be in fragments internally but not externally. And having checked his reflection once in all the mirrors, he decided to double-check. He had decided that objects were acting conspiratorially against him, that they had established a pact through which they would bring about his ruin. He returned to each mirror, this time slowly. Studiously, scrutinising his face with agonisingly close-up exposure, convinced that the mirror was incorrect in its commentary, and that he was about to catch it out in the process of distorting his image. He would find his face divided, one side youthful, the other middle-aged, but always the same fixed image was returned as his reflection.

He went back into his private black marble bathroom and increased the density of foundation on his face. It now had an impasto pigmentation, and his true features were inscrutable. He looked like an actor in grease-paint: his face was a mask. He accentuated his eyes with kohl and liked the effects. The more he exaggerated the decadent extremes of a cosmetic mask, the better he felt. He was once again situated at a remove from reality. He had maintained his ideal of the weird, even though he was conscious of effecting an illusion. He stood back from the mirror and reviewed his artistry. It would do fine, but he dreaded having to remove it before going to sleep. It would become a secret ritual, the act he would guard with impassable secrecy. He decided he would sleep in his make-up for fear of being caught out, and replace it each morning in the privacy of his locked bathroom.

Composed but deeply disquieted, he sat down to await Florentino's return. He poured himself a glass of champagne, consoling himself for his morning indulgence with the idea that it was his birthday. He could not remember how old he was. Too much had happened in the years in which he had lived in a body that had expressed unchanging youth. His way of life had erased chronology. Everything connected with his past was furred around the edges. It was like an out-of-focus photograph. But the murders he had hoped to eradicate broke through with a harrowing persistence. They came back with persistent visitation. They lived as a subtext to his life, breaking into his dreams and forcing a window in his day consciousness. He sensed that Basil Hallward was unreconciled to being dead. He had been attached to life and was too abruptly separated from being. Dorian sensed Basil's urgency to disorbit and return to earth. His brother had gone right down the tunnel, he had been assimilated into death, and when he appeared it was as a menacing hallucinated phenomenon. If Dorian encountered him in his mind, it was out walking by the jetties, when he would reveal himself as a blinding flash before receding into whatever dimension claimed him.

Dorian poured himself a second glass of champagne and thought of Harry, and of the hurt in their relationship. Harry, who had initially corrupted him, had been unable to live with his prodigy. Dorian's capacity for decadence was voracious beyond Harry's most extreme imaginings. But he missed him, even if it was hate that had substituted for love and fuelled their desperate relationship. Harry had reconverted to convention out of shock at Dorian's adoption of amoral practices. Dorian, in deciding to accept his birthday, was suddenly full of his past. It all flooded back as he sat waiting for Florentino to return. But he was determined to celebrate the person he had become. There was no going back, and he would not have wished it. He was the embodiment of his experiential journey, and he would live with that.

When Florentino returned, Dorian suspected a hint of immediately cancelled surprise in the young man's recognition of his heavily made-up face. He flinched on the inside, fearing that Florentino already knew of the vestiges of age concealed by his make-up. But Florentino was clearly disquieted by something far more disturbing than Dorian's appearance. The youth put his parcels down on a chair and stood there too distracted to speak. He was frozen into a glacial fugue. Without saying a word, he reached into his pocket and handed Dorian a sheet of paper with a nail-mark through the top. On it written in red were the stark words DORIAN GRAY – MURDERER.

'I saw him on the other side of the street, outside the shop,' said Florentino in a nervously delayed voice. 'He was looking direct at me. We can't go on like this, Dorian. Let's leave Venice. Let's get out of here.'

Florentino collapsed into a chair and Dorian could see anger in him mixed with fear. It was the unspoken anger of someone who blamed the other for the situation in which he found himself trapped. Dorian could see that Florentino was incapable of taking more but was still too frightened to leave. He poured himself a drink, but he disdained even to look at it. He was sunk into a state of morose anxiety. He looked up and reiterated his threat: 'We've got to go. We can't stay here. Let's get out now.'

Dorian wanted to say 'There's nowhere left to go. Nadja would track us from city to city.' But he bit on his words and appeared to be seriously reflecting on Florentino's urgent request for flight. In his own strategy he was deepening his inner refuge. He imagined the house developing an architectonics of labyrinthine passages, involuted mazes that could never be penetrated. The construct would enter hyperspace. It would become an artefact in the tenth dimension. Dorian would be lost in a time-warp. It was his way of eluding Nadja, but it was a means of escape that would prove unshareable with Florentino. He could twist his inner dimension to a warped infinity. He would disappear into a black hole.

'We'll go tomorrow,' he said, in the hope of allaying Florentino's fear. 'I need to make some financial preparations today. We can't just take off without making provisions.'

'Promise me we'll go tomorrow,' Florentino begged. 'I can't stand being under threat any longer. I can't bear Nadja hanging around outside all day and all night, waiting to strike. We are crazy staying here.'

Dorian listened to Florentino express his immediate fears. It was like hearing breaking glass as the youth gave voice to months of repressed rage and panic. All his loathing for his situation cracked out, tempered only by an indomitable strain of loyalty. Dorian removed himself from emotional involvement and looked objectively at the best means of manipulating Florentino into staying. He himself found it impossible to enter into the reality of the situation. An opaque sheet of glass separated him from Florentino's suffering. It interposed between him and the world. If he threw himself at the air he suspected his reflection would bounce back off the screen. He was solitary to the degree of being the only one of his species. He thought of himself as the last man. He was going nowhere. He refused to treat Nadja as a potentially fatal threat. Tomorrow, in his mind, would never come. He would extend today so that it would last for ever. The night would prove the great night. It would be full of occult marvels. Jewels would rain out of the stars, the dead would sleepwalk across the canals, and time in terms of the body-clock would cease to exist. Dorian had waited for the great night, and he had no intention of letting Florentino go on the advent of the blazingly miraculous. If they were to live through this night, they would never die. There was a perverse optimism at work in his nerves. He would sit it out and see the culmination of his work. Even the stars would fall at his instigation.

Partly reassured that they would leave tomorrow, Florentino drank his glass of champagne and busied himself about the apartment. Dorian could hear him checking on locks, his obsession with security had increased day by day.

Dorian found himself compulsively smudging his make-up with his fingertips. He kept on hoping that he would rediscover his youthful face. He drew all the curtains and lit candles. The autumn afternoon would drop early with big shadows. He knew that on such afternoons the city looked as though it had been submerged by a lake. It would be lost to an ultramarine penumbra.

Dorian would prepare books, drugs, clothes and all the accoutrements necessary to perform ritual magic. They were approaching the night, and this time it would be the last one. It would be the neurological apocalypse towards which he had worked. He listened to Florentino cleaning up in the kitchen and putting limited order into an apartment that now never received guests, and in which he had lost orientation as to the cycle of night and day. He felt that the apartment was drifting off like a wreck on the grey seas. It was no longer situated in time. It was everywhere and nowhere. He would have liked himself and Florentino to have represented the same relationship to time and space. And to have transcended all boundaries. Dorian felt the autonomous split occurring in his psyche. He was travelling away from reality. He had the idea he was on the threshold of a maze which would lead by progressive stages to the interior. There was a black angel at the entrance to the labyrinth. His eyes were gold and he wore a gold-feathered headdress. The transparent button in his navel displayed a bright blue sky on the inside. When he held out the palm of his right hand a star dazzled by way of tutelary guidance. Dorian knew that this was the messenger appointed to preside over the great night. He was the emissary who would point the way to the interior. And as suddenly as the vision had appeared, so it dematerialised. Dorian stood back from the afterglow of its departure, a piece of psychotic phenomena burning off to the world of collective imageries. He imagined the labyrinth supported by jet and malachite pillars. Guides would move fluently from passage to passage. There would be banks of television and computer screens on which the dead would show. All of the psychopathic pantheon would be there – Caligula, Heliogabalus, Pope Pius V, the Marquis de Sade, an inventory of dictators, presidents, stars, discoursing in interactive interviews about their experiences as the dead. They would be formulating the constituents of their new lives. Dorian knew that in another room Oscar Wilde would be there on screen, his humiliating sentence lifted, his dialogue loaded with aphoristic irreverence, his manner changed by the profundity of his spiritual evaluations. He would stay a long time listening to Oscar and then push on to the interior. Room by room the great would dominate the psychic channels.

Dorian was totally distracted by his vision. He saw himself walking with a jaguar on a jewelled leash behind his exotic psychopomp. Magicians would be performing rituals in secret rooms. A torrential waterfall of faces would hang suspended over the lapidary edge of an abyss. These were the new arrivals come from hospitals, the streets, motorways, the immediate discharges from the temporal. He would move on beyond their startled apprehension and encounter a congress of black angels, everything relayed on a giant screen, the ultramarine ceiling and walls lit with gold stars.

In a state of excitement Dorian moon-walked towards his bedroom. He wanted to take his portrait out of its concealment.

He knew the time was near when he would confront his ultimate destiny, and that the painting was the manifestation of his future. He had transferred it to a safe secured inside a wardrobe, concealed by a floor-to-ceiling mirror. He was confident that Florentino was making preparations for their evening celebrations. He would be arranging the table and selecting the delicacies which aroused some sort of appetite in his deadened palate. Dorian locked his bedroom door, fought with his reflection which jumped up big in the opposite wall mirror, and resolved to challenge his altered appearance through consulting the painting. He stepped into a sliding glass partition, took out a key and opened the wardrobe, and then proceeded to operate the serial to the heavy metal safe. Fear balled in his throat. He felt the adrenalin flooding his system. There was an unidentifiable smell surrounding the wraps with which the painting was protected. It was the smell of his past, of Basil Hallward's studio, of the sunlit mornings in which he had sat in that studio talking to Harry and Basil of all manner of artistic and philosophic phenomena. He inhaled his past as he had known it in London, and the first enduringly long summer in which he had grown magnetised by Harry's conversation.

He lifted the portrait out and placed it on the bed. He half expected it to explode. And faced with the prospect of confronting his catastrophic biography in the mutable effects of paint, he backed off, not daring to take the portrait out of its protective wraps. He had come so far, but he lacked the courage to continue. He watched his equivocal gestures register in the big mirror, and reassured himself that he would revert to perennial youth the moment he followed his guide into the maze. But something within him refrained from immediately appraising the painting. He needed to ritualise the act, and decided that he would do it in Florentino's company as they celebrated the great night. The youth needn't know the origins of the painting, nor whom it was originally intended to depict. Dorian would claim it was a valuable heirloom he had unearthed while sorting through things needed for their departure the next day. He intended that the portrait should serve as a symbol of apocalypse, a flagrant sign prompting their journey to the interior.

Dorian decided to dress for the occasion. He stroked a rail of velvet jackets like the sheen of a familiar cat. Greens, purples, red, blacks, cobalts. He chose a hand-sewn black one, and matched it with a white frilly shirt. With his full make-up he looked dressed for the stage. Even if he resembled a simulacrum of himself it would do to take him into the big night. And by the time he assessed the psychophysical state portrayed by the painting he would already be overtaken by the momentum that would carry him over the threshold into the marvellous possibilities to be explored in the underworld.

He thought once again of the big events in his life. Would he have been different, and would his life have pursued a different tangent, if he hadn't met Harry that summer's day in Basil Hallward's studio? There was no answer to these things. The accumulative force of his inner dynamic had been realised and would continue through his journey to self-realisation. But the big events in his life replayed themselves on inner film, like obsessions he would never escape. They were always consistent. Harry, Basil Hallward, Oscar Wilde in Paris, his half-brother, Sibyl, who had committed suicide for unrequited love. And to a lesser degree the inventory of characters he had met in his nocturnal explorations of the city. He had known so many transvestites by night who in the day reverted to singular masculine identities. And women disguised as men, who sat in smoky clubs, while a pianist followed a jazz melody to its unresolvable conclusion. He had encountered all the different ones, he had fallen down the stairs over the same repeating faces. They all came back at him with recriminative curiosity. And in his omnivorous greed for power, Dorian wanted to take them all with him into the inner kingdom. He had presided over a court and he was not going to relinquish his occult authority in another dimension. He would reclaim his retinue when the time was right, and discover a whole new following waiting for him in the maze.

He carried the portrait back downstairs, manoeuvring it with great caution. Florentino had lit candles at the big table in the dining-room, and had arranged displays of white and red carnations. A subtle Japanese incense enhanced the intimate, ceremonial atmosphere of the room. Dorian placed the portrait upright in the chair facing his seat at the opposite end of the table. He wanted to face his still concealed destiny. At a certain point he would slash the brown paper protectives from the portrait and savagely confront his counterpart.

Florentino came back into the room carrying glasses. He still looked anxious. His eyes were loaded with fear-points, as though he were on the edge of short-circuiting. Shock was written into his strained features. He clearly did not want to be there but was making a compromise in order to hold Dorian to his side of the agreement. His movements were robotic and conditioned by strain. He avoided looking at Dorian and busied himself with arranging the table. He laid the cutlery and placed glasses.

'Why are you setting places for three?' Dorian inquired, the element of surprise taking his voice up an octave.

'Because you've placed the portrait at the end of the table,' said Florentino. 'You once told me a little about it, when you were high on drugs.'

'What did I tell you?' Dorian demanded, modifying the assertion in his voice, so as not to appear dictatorial.

'I can't remember,' said Florentino. 'You said that someone had painted a portrait of you and that you didn't now dare to look at it. You said the thing was you, and you were it, or something like that.'

Dorian withdrew into himself. More of his life was known to others than he had suspected. He felt suddenly afraid at having told Florentino the true story of his life. In his out-of-it, drugged state of altered consciousness he may have given too much away. Dorian was immediately suspicious, and his sense of disquiet communicated itself to Florentino.

'I shouldn't have mentioned it,' said Florentino. 'It was just a few words you said one night when I was in your room before you fell asleep. It's nothing.'

Dorian returned to pacing around the room, his manic frustration translated into caged energies. He was like someone on overreach with nowhere to go. He mistrusted everyone but the angel standing guard on the threshold. He was still there staring directly at Dorian, his gold eyes programmed to take him to another dimension.

Dorian sat down in his chair and faced the blank rectangle of his portrait under wraps. When Florentino poured out glasses of Nuits-Saint-Georges, Dorian contemplated the isolation surrounding their preparatory initiation into the night. The celebrants were all on the other side of the threshold, assembled in orgiastic crowds in a spotlit amphitheatre. They were waiting for him to officiate over the wild extravaganza. He saw himself walking through a tunnel towards the stage, a transvestite retinue in his wake. When he arrived on the stage, an eruptive roar would reverberate like surf around the circular arena. His hieratic status would be instantly acknowledged.

Dorian noticed that Florentino was drinking with a regularity quite in contrast to his normal moderate intake. He was clearly unnerved, and needed alcohol to take the edge off his anxiety. His movements were jumbled; he looked like someone afraid he would be sprung on from behind. He presented a series of light dishes, but appeared like Dorian to be disinterested in eating.

'You have not realised the momentousness of this occasion,' said Dorian. 'We are on the edge of the great night.'

'I simply want to get through it and away tomorrow,' Florentino commented. 'I won't stay here longer than tomorrow. I'm going with you or without you.'

An impacted silence returned to the room. Florentino jumped at the sound of rain starting up outside. It sounded as though someone was throwing pebbles at the window. Each individual drop announced itself through a pinging ricochet off the glass. Florentino got up and drew aside the curtain to reassure himself that it was only rain. He returned to the table wild-eyed. He was alert to every sound that entered his neural net. For Dorian the rain had oddly comforting associations. It had been an accompanist to most of his nocturnal moves in all the big capitals. Its susurrating discourse had entered into his occult and sexual dialogues. Rain had been transmitted as a group of sound-clusters into the ambience of his most secret arts. To Dorian it seemed fitting that the rain should arrive now, driven in off the night lagoon. It would serve as a last elemental commentary on his life. It was increasing in intermittent velocity, coming and going like a visitor trying to attract attention outside in the street.

Dorian felt an irreparable gulf between himself and Florentino. They could have been sitting at opposite ends of the world, waiting for a violent surf to wash them away. Dorian was tightening into himself. He no longer wanted contact with anyone. His neurons, axons and dendrites were individuated to a point of total exclusion of all others. He knew that if he concentrated his mental energies, one single ray would shatter Florentino into unresolvable fragments. The power was building in him. It had come on like a red light in his front brain. The current was primed for optimum potential. He would use it only after he had discovered the outcome with the portrait.

Florentino nervously filled the glasses. There was a presence in the air, something like static, or someone who would not materialise but whose dynamic was registering in a series of freaky impulses. Dorian continued to review his past and to anticipate his future. A line of black angels, all bearing torches like a dance troupe and with 3D multicoloured hair, were quizzing a room just off the entry passage into the labyrinth. They were carrying a large television, on which the arrival of an important celebrity was being recorded. The object appeared to weigh nothing and to float on the hands of the four angels supporting it. Dorian could see the phased arrival staring in a confused state from the blue screen. He was attempting to adjust to the transition. His eyes were not seeing yet in the tenth dimension, but he knew it had had happened and that he was dead. There were no familiar props around him, and he was clearly amazed to be in a disembodied, gravity-free zone. Acclimatisation had not occurred. The person was like an amnesiac somnambulist, someone who had entered on the wrong side of space and was unable to return. But already he was responding to a new set of neurological vibrations. He was attuning to a postbiological ethos in which his power would be differently channelled into psychic frequencies.

Florentino got up suddenly from the table, almost overturning his chair. His face was wild with raging alarm. He went over to the dining-room door, hands out wide, toes pointing off the floor, his body propelled by fear. Then he spun round and said, 'There's someone there. I know it. Quick, let's get out of here. Let's go.'

Dorian remained unmoved. His eyes were fixed on the portrait. He would do nothing to redress Florentino's hysteria, for he considered it to be unfounded. Florentino came back to the table, but he had given up any interest in food. He was jumpy and petulant. He pushed his plate aside with a resounding clatter of cutlery. Dorian, who had always known the youth as compliantly passive, was knocked off balance by his slamming a fist down on the table. It was an unmodified projection of immediate rage. And that done, he withdrew into himself, as though he was trying to swallow the sonic disturbance and pretend it had never happened.

Dorian bit at the rim of his wineglass. He was not prepared for Florentino's coming up to him, almost soundlessly, an expression of profound compassion in his eyes. He ran a hand through Dorian's hair and said, 'What's happened? This is all like a nightmare', and Dorian knew immediately that Florentino had discovered the change in him. 'It's your hair,' said Florentino. 'It has turned grey in the course of the last hour. What is happening?'

Dorian tore himself free of Florentino. His hands flew to his head, in a move to cover the evidence of change. And he had the impression his face was sagging in the same instant. He ran to the nearest mirror. Grey hair was showing through the platinum dye. He did not recognise himself, and the person reflected there was not someone he wanted to know. The magnified caricature of everything he had most feared was staring back at him. He tilted at the mirror, pulled it off its brackets, lifted it over his head and smashed it on the floor. He stood there gasping from the exertion as the splinters detonated in a crossfire across the room.

Florentino backed off. There was a mirror on the opposite wall and he anticipated Dorian's next move, which was to repeat his action. Dorian pulled the oval mirror from its support, a mirror with an eighteenth-century gilt frame, put it on the floor and jumped on it like a diver projecting flatly, feet first, vertical into still water. The resulting crack sounded like ice thawing on a frozen river. 'I will get you all,' he threatened, treading the mirror into fractured shards.

'Don't you dare look at me,' he warned Florentino, turning his back on him and manoeuvring over to his chair at the table. Something impelled him obstinately to return to his seat confronting the portrait, as though he had still to meet with his final condemnation. He screened his face with his hands, and his grey hair streamed over his hands. He was tasting the bitter, irreversible ontology of his destiny. The youth he had believed to be his as an immutable prerogative had been turned round.

He dug his fingernails into his face, expecting blood. He was outraged that Florentino should see him old and disfigured. He could feel the outline of his face beneath the make-up. The accelerated deterioration had occurred since his first discovery of defacement earlier in the day. 'How long have I looked like this?' he screamed at Florentino. 'You allowed this to happen to me. You have stood by and watched me degenerate. I hate you for it.'

Dorian reached out blindly for an open bottle. Keeping one hand clamped to his face, he poured with the other. He drank one glass and then another in rapid succession. The residual wine streaked his damaged make-up. Two red zigzags indented in the caked base.

'Throw all the mirrors out of the house,' he shouted at Florentino. 'Even if we are only here for another night, I want them broken. Go and do it. I command you to break them!'

Dorian listened, but there was no sound of obedient footsteps, or of Florentino acting on his demands. For a moment he thought the room was empty, but through his partially closed fingers he could make out the outline and density of someone standing at the opposite end of the table. He assumed that Florentino was too shocked to obey his peremptorily phrased imperatives. Dorian sensed that Florentino had contracted into absolute stillness. He must have been paralysed by terror. There was the amplified sound of audibly regulated breathing. Dorian was preparing himself to face the portrait. In his state of physical decay he did not want to remain about much longer. He needed to follow the black androgynous angel across the threshold and assume a role of unmediated power. He wondered where amongst the dead he would encounter Basil Hallward. Would Basil be with the anonymous crowds in the amphitheatre? Would they recognise each other? Dorian knew that his transpersonal initiation would be on a much higher plane than Basil's. He had killed Basil as a means of buying time to continue his occult preparation. Basil had endangered his freedom of growth. People were not important to Dorian. They were obstructions to be removed if they should interfere with his despotic hunger for advancement.

He kept his head buried in his hands. 'Go back and break the mirrors!' he shouted again, but there were no acquiescent footsteps hurrying out of the room on the heels of his orders. He placed his head right on the table to obscure his reality. He listened again. He was sure Florentino had left the room but he dared not look up. He was saving that for the moment when he raided the portrait. He had suffered the ultimate indignity, and now he was ready for redemption.

He issued another savage directive to Florentino before retreating into a state of wordless immobility. He decided to console himself with a drink before making his attack on the painting. The liquid overspilled his glass, staining his fingers, as he crammed the contents into his mouth. He felt suddenly debased and unregenerate, but still sure of his direction. His whole life was concentrated into the red blip flashing on and off in his head. It represented a spatial connection to the dimension he was about to encounter.

In his extreme oscillation of moods, he felt sometimes the desire to be completely alone, and at others the wish to have Florentino near him. He would have to leave him behind, for Florentino was uninitiated into the secret rites of the spectacular apocalypse implied by deathlessness. Dorian reminded himself that you had to die with your eyes open and retain full expansive consciousness as you encountered the metamorphic tunnel. Florentino would have to go back into life, back into the urinous, sedimentary Venetian alleys. His place was there. He would approach death in a different way, another time. He would come to it without preparation or preconception. He would cross its threshold hoping for everything and nothing. Starlight or the void. The perfect gondolier up to his eyes in roses or a last temporal awareness of a rusty hull being torched in a shipping-yard on a desultory Sunday. Dorian's inner vision was brightening. A light had come on at the interior. Hard, luminous and cold. He would have liked to share it with Harry, the man who had run back to convention and the social cast. He kept thinking that Florentino must have been too shocked to move, and was standing stunned at the other end of the table. If he turned up the volume of psychic energy in his head, he would burn him to ash. He had disobeyed his urgent commands and would not now be taken across the threshold.

Dorian went deeper into his inner world. His vision was seething with conflicting tensions, lights were racing across his mind like shooting stars. He would get up in a moment and slash the protective covering from the portrait with a knife. He would confront himself and leave everyone behind.

He raised himself from the table. He closed his eyes so as to shut out awareness that he was being watched. It would be for only a little while. He heard his footsteps resound on the boards. He guided himself towards the portrait, knife in hand. He cut the air with the blade, all the time keeping his eyes closed. A finger tapping his shoulder had him open them in a disconnective flash. He thought he was hallucinating, for it was Nadja who was standing, elbows propped on the chair, supporting the portrait. His mouth broke into a down-twisted smile. Nadja was standing guard over his destiny. His eyes were black with malicious refutation. He had all the time in the world to wait for Dorian. He had crossed his arms in a manner resembling an indignant woman. He was indomitable like a weasel that had exhausted a rabbit's defences. And both of them had always known it would come to this. A final confrontation on the edge of death. The meeting of two flawed apotheoses. Nadja was standing there with the contained power of the indestructible. He was challenging Dorian to choose between him and the portrait; between physical and metaphysical realities. Dorian realised that Florentino must have fled the apartment. It was Nadja who had been standing there watching him for what seemed a protracted infinity of suffering. It was his adversary who was delighting in his involuntary capitulation to age, the parodic self-exposure he had feared since the first recognition of his beauty in childhood. And in a flash a day came back to him. One he had spent as a child in an autumnal morning in Norfolk. He had run away from his mother to the beginnings of mist on the marshes. He had tasted fear on his tongue, but an obdurate defiance made him refuse to turn back. His vision had been arrested by the fragments of a mirror he had discovered on the ground. He had picked up a glittering triangle and instinctively placed it in front of his face. He had managed to get an eye into focus, and that done he would not let it go. He was captivated by its green beauty. When his mother had found him, he would not let go of the mirror, he had kept on holding it to his face, and in struggling to resist, he had scratched his mother's hand with the segment. He had felt no remorse at inflicting the wound, which he knew was deliberate despite his mother's convictions that it was an accident.

Nadja made no attempt to impede his approaching the portrait. He looked disinterested, as though he was waiting to be impressed by the action. Dorian's senses were so heightened that he could distinguish every scent in the apartment. A cocktail of scents was being analysed by his right nostril, then his left. Cocaine had for so long anaesthetised his sense of smell and taste that he was amazed at this sensory rejuvenation. His diminished faculties were coming alive again. There was a buzz of electricity chasing through his nerves, a revivifying hum. He delayed his invasion of the portrait. He wanted to break out in hysterical laughter. It all seemed so easy, this process of living and dying. Neither really mattered, for both could be corrected and they were interchangeable, and he had already been inducted into a preview of death. He assumed that his powers had prevented even Nadja from killing him. He had orchestrated his own grand denouement. These minutes were to be his final act of supreme control. He too had all the time in the world compressed into his end. A microsecond could represent a year if it was magnified by the senses to a shatteringly sustained dynamic. He felt the weight of the meat-knife in his hand. For a moment he oscillated between aiming it at Nadja or the portrait. It really didn't matter. It was all the same. He already knew his status in death, and the number of his aberrations seemed irrelevant. He was a king of the underworld, a magus waiting to be crowned. He toyed with the knife again, exaggerating the mechanics of his performance, and overstating what he felt to be a unilateral supremacy. 'I'll kill you if you interfere with me,' he said laughingly to Nadja.

Nadja was still standing there without moving. Dorian could make out the flicker of his eyelashes. They were like a drumbeat in the amplified silence. He could hear the blood in Nadja's arteries. He began playfully jabbing at the brown paper protecting the portrait. He gave it lateral slashes, incisions that deepened with each cross-hatching of the blade. He was shredding the protective, ripping it to tatters. He was slicing at himself with the potential to kill, splitting the protective skin in which his identity was concealed. There was a light around him that touched everything he did; he felt himself to be illuminated by numinous mystery. A sharp cutting tear, and another in quick succession, and the paper split off in shaved peelings. He was almost there. It needed only one more incisive cut, a cut that could occupy a minute or a year or a lifetime. He wondered if Nadja was there, his eyes fixed on the knife, or if he was hallucinating a simulacrum of his blackmailing adversary. He pulled back from his knife-point artistry. The black angel with the gold eyes was still standing guard on the threshold. The gold plumes in his headdress were perfectly still. The rain had come back outside with punctuated flurries tipping the window. It was like a conciliation for having lived. The pure elemental rain sparkling in its descent from the night sky.

Dorian closed his eyes and tore at the last of the protective clinging to the portrait. In his mind he had expected to encounter a putrefying, bleeding organism, the facial absorbent of all the evil he had perpetrated in life. His last sight of the painting had shown him the satanic geography of this psyche. He had confronted his maniacally perverse double. All the accumulated corruption that had never registered in his permanently youthful face had been evident in the painting. But now what he encountered was the exact reverse. The Dorian staring back at him was the golden-haired youth whom Basil Hallward had depicted in the summer in which he had sat for the portrait. It was he who was old and who embodied the catastrophic physical blemishes that had grown to be the painting's biographical identity. He could hear Nadja's cold, ironically impersonal laughter crowd the room with its triumphant sadism. It was only seconds before the concealed blade hit. He could not tell if he fell direct into Nadja's arms or if the angel had turned him round to begin his journey to the centre of the underworld.